Under the
Storyteller's Spell

UNDER THE STORYTELLER'S SPELL

An Anthology of Folk-tales
from the Caribbean

Edited by Faustin Charles

Illustrated by Rossetta Woolf

VIKING KESTREL

VIKING KESTREL

Published by the Penguin Group
27 Wrights Lane, London w8 5 tz, England
Viking Penguin Inc., 40 West 23rd Street, New York, New York 10010, USA
Penguin Books Australia Ltd, Ringwood, Victoria, Australia
Penguin Books Canada Ltd, 2801 John Street, Markham, Ontario, Canada l3r 1b4
Penguin Books (NZ) Ltd, 182–190 Wairau Road, Auckland 10, New Zealand

Penguin Books Ltd, Registered Offices: Harmondsworth, Middlesex, England

First published 1989
10 9 8 7 6 5 4 3 2 1

Filmset in Linotron Trump Mediaeval by
Rowland Phototypesetting Ltd, Bury St Edmunds, Suffolk
Printed in Great Britain by Richard Clay Ltd, Bungay, Suffolk

A CIP catalogue record for this book is available from the British Library

ISBN 0–670–82276–0

CONTENTS

ACKNOWLEDGEMENTS

I WOULD LIKE to thank the following people who most generously gave me their advice and encouragement: Jean Popeau and Petronella Breinburg for their enthusiastic response to the whole idea; Pedro Pérez Sarduy for his invaluable assistance in finding the work of Alfredo Arango Franco; Bridget Jones for her kind comments and help in tracking down the work of Alex-Louise Tessonneau, and Barbara Bulmer-Thomas for her help in finding the work of Elwood Fairweather.

Faustin Charles

INTRODUCTION

B ETWEEN NORTH and South America lie the islands and territories of the English, Spanish, French and Dutch-speaking Caribbean.

From this large area I have chosen eighteen folk-tales for this anthology.

Caribbean folk-tales are based on myths and legends which are either African, European, East Indian or Amerindian, the native culture of the Caribbean. Some of them can be traced back to one culture, while others combine two or more of these folk traditions. It is this wide variety that makes the Caribbean one of the richest areas in the world for its folk-tales.

Some myths and legends are known in one form or another in different territories of the Caribbean. 'Anancy', the spider-man of West African origin is, for example, popular throughout the English-speaking Caribbean. Then there is 'La Diablesse', a devil-woman who appears in a tale from Martinique, but who is known in all the other French-speaking territories, and in some English-speaking ones as well.

There are certain traditional ways of story-telling in the Caribbean world and these ways have been incorporated in the stories of this anthology. A storyteller, like the one in 'Tata Dohende', uses gesture, mime, song and dance in the narration of his tale. Skilfully the storyteller transports his or her listeners into the world of fantasy; it almost seems as if a spell is cast over them. The storyteller will often start or end a tale by saying 'Crick!' to which the listeners have to answer 'Crack!' (In the French-speaking countries it is 'Krick!' and 'Krack!' or 'Kwik!' and 'Kwak!')

Rhymes are also important in the telling of a story. 'The Gaulin Wife', for example, ends with:

Biddy bo ben
Go to where flamingoes fly
And ask them to disprove this lie.

In another tale, 'The Little Girl Saved by her Father', the storyteller ends with the following lines:

And that's where they gave me one little kick
Right out of the basket and into the bottle.

Thus, in the Caribbean, it is not only the story which draws the reader into a world of magic, but also the way in which the story is told.

The setting further adds to the beauty of the event of storytelling, as it is more widespread in rural than in urban areas, and as it is usually done on a full moon night.

Faustin Charles

TATA DOHENDE

(from Belize)

ELWOOD FAIRWEATHER

T HE TOWN where Louis lived was surrounded by jungle and hills. A river ran by on the eastern side; it was dark, deep and quiet. Wooden houses of varying sizes straggled along the riverbank a few hundred yards from the water's edge. They were built on stilts to escape the ravages of the flood waters when the rainy season came. The eight hundred or so families who lived there earned their bread in the timber industry or by working the land in a small way.

Louis thoroughly enjoyed the life of the town. He often watched, fascinated, as the huge trucks hauling giant mahogany trees passed through his town on their way to the river where they floated downstream, lashed together into massive rafts, all the way to the sea. Thence to be shipped to England and other parts of Europe. The thing Louis loved most, however, were the nights when the electric lights of the town had gone off and the grown-ups gathered round the kerosene lamp to spin yarns. Louis had to keep very quiet and still so as to escape the notice of his parents, who would surely have sent him to bed had they been aware of him crouching there, deep in the shadows.

Saturday nights were different of course, for then
everybody, even Mary, his little sister who was
barely five years old, was welcomed into the
charmed circle around the lamp.

In particular, Louis liked to hear time and again
the stories of Tata Dohende. Hearing the adults
tell of Daddy Dohende and his exploits always sent
delicious shivers of fear chasing down his spine.
In Louis' opinion, the best storyteller of all was a
man called Ken. Ken from Kendal he called himself. Almost everyone shared this high opinion of
Ken's storytelling. Even the adults who chuckled
and winked and called Ken a liar, were amused and
often spellbound by his tales. The storyteller from
Kendal seemed to take pleasure in appearing at
Louis' house at least one night each week to spin
yarns. It was Saturday nights Louis liked best,
when rum passed round the adults and there was
never a shred of a thought of school next day in
anyone's head, not even his parents thought of it.
Knowing this, Ken would tell two or maybe three
stories if they were lucky. Sometimes he would
even tell all he knew about Tata Dohende. On
these rare occasions the misty, grey dawn would
steal up the river and find him still at it.

Ken was easily the tallest man around; skinny,
lithe and supple like the brown swathes of the ti-ti
vines festooning the ancient trees in the nearby
forest. He was a born storyteller, steeped in the
folklore tradition of the 'old heads', the great grand-
mothers and grandfathers of a past time who lived
now only in memory. He had much in common
with great storytellers everywhere. Ken never told
a story the same way twice. The spell he cast over
his audience with his tale would grow like a living
thing. Although it was Ken who told the stories,

they were, in a sense, the creation of all present – they were the dreams and fears of his audience. From minute to minute he was very sensitive to the slightest shadow of feeling coming from the people seated around him. With that kind of inspiration he wove his tale and would choose his words and even the gist of his story to squeeze every bit of drama from the situation. With eerie shadows cast by the low flame of the lamp, he would whisper chillingly, 'and so Tata Dohende tied the boy to a tree and prepared a huge cauldron of boiling water for his evening meal. It was a long time since Tata Dohende had had a boy to eat!'

It was Ken's description of Dohende which drove fear into Louis' heart, and yet made the boy long for more. According to Ken, Tata Dohende was a manlike creature living in the jungle. He was hairy all over like a monkey, and the unique thing about him was that his feet were turned backwards. This, Ken explained, was to fool any man who wanted to track Dohende. They would follow his footprints and go in the opposite direction. Dohende wore a wide-brimmed hat three feet across, and his constant companion was a rooster who spat fire when he crowed. He liked to lure children into the forest; he lured them with his rooster into the forest where they would get lost and he would capture them and eat them.

There was one particular Dohende story, told not only by Ken but also by many others, which all the adults seemed to believe in. Ken's eyes bulged whenever he related this Dohende story. 'Yes,' he would say in answer to the anxious questions of the children round him, 'I saw it with my own eyes!' These words would draw forth signs of regret from the boys and girls, because bloody as the story was, many still wished they had been there to witness the strange things he described.

One particular Saturday night in response to cries of, 'Heave along shore!' and 'Story! Story!', Ken went into great detail.

'Everyone know how Tata Dohende is a short little man,' he said, indicating with his hand a height above ground of barely three feet. Now he broke into Creole, the kind of English that people spoke thereabouts.

'Well mek a tell you, 'e look stupid wearing dat big hat too. I see 'im comin' down de road sometimes wen 'e don't see me. I live off the land but I am a hunter too. I know the bush like de back a me han'. Dohende fast, but now an' again I faster dan 'im. When I fix dese eyes on him he can't pull dat disappearing trick on me. An' I'm not afraid. No siree! The moment he knows I see 'im 'e ducks right back into the bush. He won't come after me! 'e only goes after cowards and lil' children.' Asked why he didn't shoot Dohende on the few occasions he saw him, Ken would reply,

'Because I tell you, he is fast! When I see him it is only a second before he spots me. If I blink he is gone. It is just as if he doesn't use his feet to escape. I wouldn't have time to shoot him. By the time my gun reached me shoulder Dohende would be a mile away. You know, sometimes I reach a spot in the jungle and I know he was just there. I can smell him and feel the breeze from him. "Ah! you saw me first, you scallywag," I would say. No, he hates to cross my track. But all this came before . . .' Here he trailed off into silence and took a sip from his glass.

'You know, when Dohende stole that girl . . . Ugh! That blinkin' creature had some nerve!

Imagine carrying off a girl of humankind and keeping her a prisoner! All she had for company was that ugly hairy thing that half the people don't believe exist. Can you imagine that? Well! But the strange thing is that God works in mysterious ways. Why did he make it so long before anybody found out? We all thought Rosalita was dead or eaten by a tiger or had ended up lost. Some said Dohende got her; these were the ones who believed. Many people don't believe Dohende exist. Mind you, all this happened a long, long time ago. Those were the days of the dug-outs and paddling *dories*;* when there were no trucks and no aeroplanes.'

Lighting a cigarette and watching for a moment the silvery clouds of smoke melt into the blackness beyond the gentle glow of the kerosene lamp on the table, he continued:

'Rosalita was the schoolteacher here. Oh, my! WAS she pretty! She had hair down to her waist, shiny and black like the seed from a *mammee apple*.† Her skin was brown and smooth like this orchid,' and he nodded towards the magnificent tiger orchid whose blossoms tumbled in joyous profusion over the rails of the veranda where they were seated. He went on:

'And she could sing, man! When she sang those old-time songs it charmed even Anancy, the big black spider in his hole. She was about twenty-five years old when she disappeared, but she looked much younger than that. Sometimes, when she was swimming in the river with those children she was teaching, she looked just like one of them.

---

* *dories*: fishing boats
† *mammee apple*: large yellow pulped fruit

Anyway, one day she did not come to school and she could not be found anywhere. Search and search we did, every inch of the place, but we had to give up in the end. We had a memorial service for her in that same church over there.' He gestured vaguely towards the wall of the blackness of the night pressing close upon them.

'But the sight of Dohende's daughter would have shocked even the *faciest** of you. Half man, half Dohende! This little girl was already three years old when we found out, and that was because Dohende decided to move out of his cave and build a hut. He must have thought, "I am like humankind now, with a beautiful wife and a family; let me build a house like humans." That rascal is probably back there now in the darkest, deepest cave he can find after his dreadful deed. Imagine, spoiling that poor girl's life by making her live with a brute!

'Glad to say I was not the one to find it out. I didn't believe it at first because it was mere boys, boys your own age who brought the news. Folks thought they were just playing the fool, so we smiled and laughed it off. That is until the time came for us big ones to see it too. Lordy! It was Alan who saw it, the whole Dohende family together; he came running to me as if Dohende was after him!

'"Ken!" he yelled. "Get your gun, man. Get your gun and rouse the neighbours!"

'I calmed him down till I could get some sense out of him. Then he told me his story and I believed him.

'"Now I bet you believe the stories I tell you!" I said to him, because he was always telling me

* *faciest*: boldest

that God would punish me for my lies whenever I
told him about things I see in the bush. Dohende
was just a fairytale to him "till that day".

'Well, half a dozen of us got together to hunt
Daddy Dohende. Alan said he saw them when they
stole a bunch of bananas from his plantation. His
banana grove is buried in the deep jungle to save
his fruit from you *pic'nie*.* So, he was just about
to enter an open clearing where he'd built a shed
when he saw the Dohende family just leaving. Mr
Dohende, short as he was, carried an enormous
bunch of bananas balanced on his hat. What a
sight! His wife and child followed behind, that is
how Alan saw it.

'We agreed they would come back to that spot
at some time for free food. All we had to do was
bide our time; as the old-time saying goes, "Every
day devil help thief, one day God help the watchman." The plan was to take Dohende's wife and
child away from him. Even to kill him if he gave
us trouble. But I tell you, when we saw the baby,
not a man wanted to touch her. Anyway, we
waited. We knew Dohende was not a night creature; too many people had seen him in the daytime.
He would come, of that we were certain. He and
his family.'

'But what did the little girl look like?' Louis
asked impatiently. 'Were her feet turned backwards like Dohende, or frontwards like Rosalita?'

'One and one,' came the immediate reply
from Ken. 'One foot turned backwards and one
frontways.'

'How could she walk like that?' a voice asked.

'Was she hairy like her father or peeled like her

---

* *pic'nie*: children

mother?' another voice piped up from the back.

'Half and half,' Ken replied eagerly, evading the first of the two questions put to him.

'And didn't you say Daddy Dohende was fast and stronger than ten men?' joined in the littlest girl present.

'Ah! But he knows what a gun is! Dohende knows the power of the gun,' replied Ken. 'He has lived around mankind long enough to know. Anyway, we waited for him in the bush at the edge of the clearing. He would come from the forest on the opposite side. He and his family. Just picture Dohende in that silly hat, and not a stitch of clothing on except for his thick covering of hairs. He had his famous cockerel with him. I don't know how he didn't smell us. He is an animal and we were up wind.

'It was then that we saw the face of the woman. What a shock we had to see it was Rosalita, who had disappeared all those years ago. She was still a great beauty and she wore some kind of clothing she had cobbled together from leaves or bark. The child following behind was as naked as the day it was born and looked to be about three years old.

'They took their time, clearing a path for the child as they went along. They had their mind on that and did not see us until they came near to the shed where Alan stored his fruit. The rooster sounded the warning; he cackled and crowed his burst of fire. Dohende glanced in our direction and took to his heels the moment he clapped eyes on us.

'This happened before we sprang from the bushes. Well, I tell you, this is one time his disappearing act didn't work. Rosalita picked up the child and ran behind him, but she couldn't make it. I fired a shot over their heads, the damn rooster flew into the air with a rattle of noises, and in the confusion Rosalita dropped the child. Dohende stopped to pick up the child, and then quickly ran into the jungle, leaving his stolen mate behind. We caught up with Rosalita and grabbed her. She seemed terrified of us, and fought like a wild thing. We looked in every bush for Dohende, but he had vanished. So we brought Rosalita home for the nurse to look after. She was so changed. She never spoke a word, just held her head and wept.'

'But what about the child?' This was from Louis again, believing Ken's story had come to an end. Ken took a sip of rum from his glass and mused silently for a while.

'Well that is another long story,' he said. 'I'll save it for another night.'

'Please, Ken?' a girl pleaded, 'Tell us about it now.'

'Well,' he spoke slowly as if thinking, 'I'll make a long story short. Don't blame me.' He said it as if to imply it would be disappointing.

'Well, many days and weeks passed after we captured the girl,' he began. 'Some of us had forgotten about Tata Dohende. What we didn't know was that the beast was waiting and hoping that Rosalita would return to him. Don't you worry. Not a mother's daughter was allowed far from home in case the same thing happened to her as it did to poor Rosalita. After about two months, Dohende got angry and came back to get his revenge — the vile brute.' Suddenly, Ken stopped talking and stared into the blackness of the night. He breathed heavily and said in a voice that sounded as if it came from deep down inside him, 'No children, I can't tell you about it.'

'Please tell us about Dohende's revenge, I beseech you!'

'We grown-up folk have to keep something for ourselves, you know,' he replied when they begged and protested. He and the children sat in the light around the table while the big folks sat on chairs in the darkness of the veranda.

'Give him another drink so he can dream up the rest,' a man's voice said in the darkness, and the others all laughed.

'*Fool de talk, but da no fool de listen,*'* another said in Creole.

'Don't you listen to them, children. Everything I tell you is the truth, and the only reason they don't want me to tell you is that they think you'll have nightmares. Heave along shore!

'The whole town was dead to the world that morning when Santos ran, hollering, along the main street. He carried something wrapped in banana leaves in his hand. A big something. He couldn't stop hollering. Everybody rushed out to see what the commotion was all about. Finally, Mr Jim the policeman came and quietened him down. Then he showed them what was in the package. He said he found it on the road near the river. I tell you, boy, the women screamed and the men backed off at the sight. It was Dohende's revenge for us taking Rosalita away from him. He had cut the child in half, right down the middle from head to toe. He kept the hairy half and gave us the human half. Mr Jim wrapped the half body in a blanket and carried it through the town to the doctor's.

* *Fool de talk, but da no fool de listen*: a fool talks, but those who listen are not fools

'When they got there, he placed his burden down on the table, ever so gently, as if it were an egg which he was afraid might break.

'The crowd pressed close to get a better look and as Mr Jim threw back the ends of the blanket, a gasp of utter astonishment and disbelief ran round the crowd.' Here Ken paused for another sip of rum, then went on:

'There on the table sitting up as if nothing had happened was Dohende's daughter made whole again, in perfect human form. She was the spitting image of her mother except she had a tuft of hair on her forehead, a cow-lick, and eyes as green as the sheen on a rooster's feathers.' Ken ended his tale and there was a long pause interrupted by deep sighs from all the children.

After everyone had gone home, Louis bombarded his father with questions, but his father gave only one reply:

'My son,' he said, 'even though Ken said he saw these things with his own eyes, you must remember that this all happened a long, long time ago, even before Ken was born. You can say it all happened before time. Remember the old saying, *"dis ya time no stan' like befo' time!"'*

---

* *dis ya time no stan' like befo' time*: The present time is not as strange and miraculous as the past time, the once-upon-a-time world

PANYA JAR

(from Jamaica)

JAMES BERRY

DUSK OF evening had come down. The oven-like warm village square had become busy with people in their work and after-work clothes. Washed and changed out of their own sweaty work clothes, Mr Kayjay, Cousin Buddy and Mr Mackey had come and sat together on a log seat near the mango tree.

The three friends enjoyed their evening drink of rum. They sipped their neat rum, sweating. Even when ice came on weekends, they still drank their white rum without ice or anything else. The men talked, sipping between. As they talked, happenings of the day began to remind them of things they lacked: something their homes lacked, their work and fields lacked, their lives, and all their senses of achievement lacked. They began to lament over drought, over poor crops of bananas and yams, over disease that rotted the hearts of their coconut trees, over their lost battles against the fierce heat of the sun, over uncheckable hurricanes and rain floods, over government promises never kept, over their never satisfied lifelong yearnings.

Mr Kayjay suddenly sighed and said, 'If only – if only – I could find that Panya Jar.'

The sound of the word 'Panya Jar' changed the men's mood like an incredible magic. A sudden silence struck them. But it was also a strange excitement that seized them. And that one remark plunged the men deep into the mysteries of the near-man-size jar of treasures, and the wealth it promised.

Most people believed the Jar existed. Because of that, usually, there wasn't anybody to say it may not exist at all. Now the men left that side out as well. But Mr Kayjay pointed out that if the Jar did exist, it certainly was tricks-master at artful hiding. Or else, it must have a magic that threw its seekers off the trail each and every time. Maybe the Jar even knew that to successfully find it, every move had to be totally perfect.

Cousin Buddy reminded Mr Kayjay, 'We all know you don't believe in a dream anyway. You don't believe in a dream and never will.'

'Not because I don't believe in dream, it mean I don't believe in riches. Is jus that I think if I goin find that Jar I goin find it by accident when I just diggin mi land.'

'Then you stand only one man to think the Jar will come like that,' Mr Mackey said.

'I don't say the Jar will come like that, I say is the one way I miself can wish it.' And, determined to make it clear how and why he didn't believe in dreams, Mr Kayjay went on protesting against not being understood.

His friends beside him simply kept on and on pouring out talk to convince Mr Kayjay. They wanted him to see that a poor man had no chance of getting wealth except through luck in a gamble. And, even so, he may well have to work and work at that game of gamble. Yet, all the time,

Mr Mackey and Cousin Buddy were well aware
they'd kept quiet about whether they'd dreamed
of the Jar and acted on it or not.

A jar-dreamer stayed silent about a dream, you
see. A jar-dreamer merely secretly looked for the
Jar at the place where the dream had shown. When
the Jar wasn't found you still kept the whole matter a secret. That way you might well get another
dream – another chance to know the spot where
the treasure Jar lay hidden.

Darkness thickened. The gaslamp of the grocery
shop was lit. The lamp's edge of light arched itself
across the men's thighs and cut them in two with
a line of shadow. Their top halves in darkness,
shifting and gesturing, the men went on excitedly,
going over puzzling old stories about the elusive
Jar. And it haunted them, kept them lost in dreams,
talking on and on . . .

You see, two stories handed down had survived
and they explained how the Jar happened to be
hidden.

One story had come from the swift way the
Spaniards had been packed off and dispatched by
the British when they'd invaded Jamaica in 1655.
The Spaniards had been so firmly settled on the
Island for 146 years they hadn't at all expected an
attack. Surprised, without defence, the Spaniards
surrendered to the British, and were given a very
short time to clear out of Jamaica for good. The
story went that the Spaniards kept valuables in
very big earthenware jars that travelled in wooden
cases. And, with no real alternative, some rich
Spaniards hurriedly buried valuables or hid them
in caves. They all firmly believed they'd return,
recapture Jamaica and resettle. But that didn't happen at all. The British didn't let them. So, because

by language use locally the word 'Spanish' got changed to 'Panya', the Panya Jar legend was made.

Now with the other story – that had come along from a different source altogether. Yet, it was equally strong, if not stronger. It had come from the days when the Caribbean waters were pirate-infested. As a way of life, the sea robbers attacked, wrecked and plundered ships and escaped with valuable cargoes.

A certain pirate captain had come into his planned-for biggest and richest day, this story said. He and his men, on a high heaving sea, attacked a ship. Their pirate clubs and guns and knives flashed on and on, killing and wounding the ship's crew. The pirates left the robbed ship battered up – a ghost ship drifting, its dead and wounded on board. And, taking care not to be sea-policed, out-gunned and caught, the pirate captain and a small crew rowed the special booty – which was the Panya Jar – ashore! There, the captain waited for the moon to come up.

To his wonderful surprise, on opening it up and examining the Jar's contents, the pirate master found more cut and uncut gems than he ever expected. Carefully packed in layers were pearls, diamonds, gold. In glorious colours of stones, all kinds of star-like jewels glittered before his eyes. All adornments – precious things – he well knew, for kings, queens, princesses and princes and ladies and gentlemen of court and high society!

Slowly, the moon came up.

The pirate captain had the Jar securely but quickly hidden – to stay there, for a time, with its brilliant rainbow layers. Then, the pirate master drew his gun unexpectedly. Bang! bang! His gun blasted down two of his crew. A black sailor and

a white one fell dead beside the hidden Jar. 'Spirits,
guard this Jar and its jewels till I return,' the captain
said. 'Only when I return for the rustless pieces
will you be free to go.' But, the story went, the
pirate chief never returned. And desperate to get
released from their duty, the spirits of the sailors
come to sleeping heads offering them the Jar.

A jar-dream should be kept secret. That was both
the door and the key to the treasure. But – with
people being people – some dream stories were
leaked out over the years.

It was known that a black priest in a black cloak
had appeared in somebody's dream. The priest
beckoned and led the dreamer to a spot where he
carefully laid crosses and a rosary on the ground.
He then showed him the great wide sea and
disappeared. Next day, the man went where the
rosary and crosses were laid on the shoreline.
He dug up the ground deep down. Nothing was
found.

Known bits of another dream revealed how a
weary and ragged white sailor appeared on the sea
coast and said, 'Follow my light footsteps.' The
dreamer followed. And taken to a rocky part of the
coastline, he watched the sailor sit down on a
rock. Then he was gone. With the dream still clear
in mind, the dreamer began many days of solo
excavation and search at and around the place
where the dreamed sailor had sat.

It was said that acting on a dream, an unidenti-
fied villager once sat alone in his canoe in moonlight from midnight to dawn, waiting for the Jar to
float; that on a hilltop in the brightness of midday
sun, a woman waited listening for the voice of a
certain bird which would lead her to a certain spot;
that in the darkness of night in a clustered palm

tree gully, another woman watched the squinting
lights of fireflies to receive a signal in the lights;
that at midnight, a man waited sea-splashed beside
coastline rocks, waiting for a light to come and
settle on a chosen rock.

Stories told how a man – totally alone – would
spend midnight to dawn digging in caves, cutting
or breaking rocks with his pickaxe and sledge-
hammer, or digging down into sand only to
come to the broad back of another rock deeply
buried.

Yet, failure to find the Jar was always a well-kept
disappointment. Failure meant that the dream had
been interpreted badly or that the information it
gave had been partly forgotten or missed in some
way. In spite of it all, the hope of luck with a
Panya Jar-dream remained the big promise of a
miracle-fortune.

There, in the village square, the three men kept
wiping their faces more regularly now. They
sweated partly from the heat of day hanging
thickly on the night air, partly from the strong
rum they drank, but mostly from their excited talk
about the tricky ways of jar-dreams, the places the
Jar could be, and oh the wealth that could be had
from the Jar!

'Africa-loot hide away in that dey Jar,' Mr Kayjay
said.

'You talk facts, brother. The facts,' Cousin
Buddy said.

'Facts no judge would utter,' Mr Mackey said.
'Yet, it all true-true.'

'All the same,' Mr Kayjay went on, 'just if ever
– if ever you should get it, what you think you
would do with Panya Jar things break down in
cash?'

'Well. Well. Fo me,' Cousin Buddy said, 'I'll tell you. You know I was in town to pay taxes.'

'Yeh.'

'Well – quite a simple thing happen. Payin mi taxes, I see the taxes clerk go and switch on a *lectric** fan. And I tell you, I sudden-sudden see I never put on a lectric switch in all mi fifty year o life. Now – gi-me Panya Jar treasure. Straightaway a lectric house. All lectric! I put up a house thas all lectric! Lectric light everywhere. Lectric icebox. Lectric everything. That would-a be mi heaven! Then – I change every way I work and cultivate the land.'

'Me too,' Mr Mackey said. 'First thing, a new big roomy house. A new bed fo mi wife. Then, a new piece o land. A tractor-and-plough. And ten heifers – to raise fo milk.'

Mr Kayjay was quiet. 'And you, Kayjay?' Cousin Buddy said.

'Well – I not a jar-dreamer as you know. But, if money should come mi way – first thing, a cement water tank to hold rain water. University fo mi grandchildren. Then, a trip to Barbados and Trinidad and Cuba. Just to see the place them and hear the people talk. As you know, like youself, I never step off we island here. I never seen a new land. I never seen another way of life . . .'

The men got up. Each one turned and went his separate way home, swallowed by the darkness of a road and then clustered leafy lanes. Two of the men particularly were quietly excited. The Jar had bewitched them and the bewitchment was comforting to them; it subdued their despair and gave them hope.

* *lectric*: electric

The night moved on as it usually did – marked here and there with the barking of dogs, the mooing of a cow, the braying of a donkey or the neighing of a horse.

Dawn came. Cocks crowed frenziedly all around the village. The sea splashed against shore walls of rocks or ran free to be spent on sand.

Under arched coconut-palm limbs that moved in a slow wind, Mr Mackey and Cousin Buddy came face to face suddenly. Both men carried a pickaxe and a machete. Appearing from opposite ends of the coastline foot track, the men surprised each other.

Cousin Buddy chuckled, 'You up early.'

Mr Mackey chuckled back. 'I was goin to say the same to you.'

'Night fishin, then?'

'Same as you.'

Each knew neither man was going to breathe a single word about his night's experience.

All to himself, Cousin Buddy would keep the night's happenings that tricked, frightened and confused him.

As his dream had showed, he'd waited at the side of the rugged platform of rocks; it projected from land into the sea conveniently. He'd stood there getting sea-sprayed. Suddenly, in a canoe-like craft near the undercliffs, two men, cloaked and faceless, had appeared. One moment the craft with the figures was there on his left – bobbing up and down on the moonlit sea. Then – in a blink – it was there on his right! And, in a performance now, the boat went switching left to right, right to left, left to right and right to left. Till, suddenly, there were two boats on each side of him, each with two figures, all looking exactly the same. And, the figures began to get out of the boats into the sea. Then, in a flash, boats, figures – the lot – were gone! Only the moonlit sea was there, bobbing up and down at the undercliffs.

'What happen?' Cousin Buddy had whispered to himself. 'Good God! What mystery this? What did the ghosts want to say? How can an ordinary man work out they puzzle? How can he know . . . ? How can he?' Then Cousin Buddy had realized he couldn't say how long he'd stayed there fixed, sea-splashed, looking at the cloaked and faceless figures in a craft. Neither could he make out how long he'd stayed there afterwards, pondering. He'd shaken his head and moved. A strange new feeling had filled him. Stepping down from the rocky seawall he'd found himself thinking how the sea was a vast ocean spreading side-to-side, forming the shores of different countries like different worlds. Then images of distances, ocean depths, ghosts, mysterious happenings, searching for wealth, all came tumbling one after the other in his head. The images went round and round, repeating, colliding, holding his attention, like an absorbing confusion. But what did it all mean? Yet it felt good – like a vision – something with a power to watch and see what it revealed. 'Distances' and 'ocean depths' sometimes came together. But what exactly did it all mean? He'd have to see. He'd have to see eventually what was revealed. He'd just have to wait and see . . .

For Mr Mackey, he knew he had to go and ponder on why nothing had happened for him – at the exact spot he'd seen the previous night in his dream. He knew, there was something about his dream he simply hadn't done right. Something he hadn't done right!

'So, no luck,' Cousin Buddy said.

'No luck. Same as you. Better luck next time.'

'Better luck next time.'

The cocks were crowing fast-fast competitively in the dawn, and the men walked away home – separately.

ME CAMOUDI

(from Guyana)

GRACE NICHOLS

EVERYWHERE Abiola walked, people turned their heads to stare at her. She was beautiful in truth and carried herself like a princess. Dark skin glowing, eyes flashing, braids jigging from a bunch behind her proud neck, and when she smiled it was like being hit by a cool sea breeze in the brilliant sunshine.

Well, with such looks it was easy to understand why nearly all the young men in the village wanted to marry her. But Abiola was headstrong and had her own ideas about the kind of man she wanted to marry.

'I want to marry the perfect man,' she always said. 'He must be handsome, clever and have a lot of money.' That was her idea of perfect.

None of the young men in the village could be considered handsome, clever and rich, all at the same time like that, and everyone who came to her door she turned away. Either he was handsome but too poor, or he was rich but too stupid, or he was clever but too ugly. It was always 'too' something, and sometimes she would have a good laugh behind their backs.

'But look at that stumpy-foot one, eh, Mammy, saying he want to marry me.'

34

But her mother only said, 'You so choosey-choosey. You going pick and choose and pick and choose till you pick and choose trouble.'

Abiola would smile her sea-breeze smile and say, 'Until I find the perfect man, I'm content to make my baskets and lie beside the sea.'

And that was just what she did most of the time; sit under her favourite coconut tree, weaving her pretty baskets and watching the soft lash of the foaming sea.

But there was a young fisherman called Tomo whom Abiola found herself becoming fond of in spite of her pledge. He came towards her one afternoon after pulling his small fishing boat up on to the shore and Abiola was struck by his strong slim looks and his serious dark eyes.

Tomo had, of course, fallen in love with Abiola and brought her gifts of fresh fish. But even though she allowed him to walk with her sometimes when she went to market to sell her baskets, the proud girl would never dream of marrying someone as poor as Tomo. He just made enough money to live on from the fish he sold.

Then Abiola found the man of her dreams. One day, a glittering carriage drew up in front of her house and out stepped the finest looking man she had ever seen. He was dressed in a costly striped suit, shiny leather shoes and a felt hat. Abiola couldn't believe he was one of her suitors.

She listened as he spoke to her father and mother in the living room, telling them all about his big estate and beautiful home, which he said was a few villages away. When Abiola came out he presented her with a box of the most exquisite pearls she had ever seen. Then he began to speak of all manner

of learned things. Well, Abiola readily agreed to
marry him.

When he left she hugged her mother, exclaiming,
'Oh, Mammy he is the man I've been waiting for.
He is the perfect man I want to marry. He look
perfect. He talk perfect. I can hardly wait to see
his estate.'

Abiola's mother and father were relieved that at
long last the girl had found someone she wanted
to marry, and they began the wedding preparations
almost at once.

As the day of the wedding drew near, a strange
sadness settled over Abiola's heart. She could not
put Tomo out of her thoughts no matter how
hard she tried. But there was no turning back
now. Wedding cake, wines, wedding gown, were
all ready and waiting. Abiola told herself not
to be stupid now that she had found the perfect
husband.

As for Tomo, he was so stricken with grief
that for days he hadn't been able to take his
boat out to sea. The day of the wedding came at
last and all the guests turned up for the feasting
and dancing. Everyone was amazed to see Tomo
there, sitting by himself in a corner. No one
could believe he would torture himself so.
Abiola in particular could not bear to look into
his eyes.

The eating and dancing were in full swing when
Tomo suddenly got up and drew Abiola's mother
aside. Tomo had been following the movements
of the charming new husband, who was smiling
and being gracious to all the guests.

Abiola's mother, who was busy looking after
the guests, seemed a bit impatient. 'What's the
matter?' she demanded.

'It's your new son-in-law,' said Tomo; 'there's
something wrong with the man.'

'Something like what?' asked the mother in
amazement.

'Well, his eyes,' said Tomo, 'they have a green-
ish, sleepy look that don't look too natural to
me.'

'For heaven's sake, Tomo,' Abiola's mother cried
out in a vexed voice. 'You just have to accept the
fact that Abiola is married now,' and she flounced
away.

Well, at last the time came for the couple to
leave for their new home. With tear-filled eyes
Abiola kissed her mother and father goodbye. She
had a sudden feeling to grab Tomo's hand and
run out of the house, but her smiling handsome
husband was holding on to her arm tight and leading her to the carriage.

The journey was a long one. The glittering carriage sped along the dusty road, leaving Abiola's
village far behind. The longer they travelled, the
lonelier and rougher the road became. The sun
disappeared behind the trees and the trees themselves threw dark shadows. Abiola was just beginning to think they'd never reach the estate, when
her husband began to bring the carriage to a halt.
Abiola looked around her in surprise.

It was a lonely *backdam** place with not an
estate or a beautiful house in sight. All she could
see in the distance was a small tumbledown shack
surrounded by tall bushes and muddy water. Suddenly Abiola went cold. Surely this couldn't be the
home of her posh husband. She told herself there
must be some mistake and turned to ask him in a

* *backdam*: ramshackle

trembling voice, 'Where is the estate and beautiful home you talked about?'

'There it is my dear,' answered her husband in his smooth voice, pointing to the shack. And this time when Abiola gazed at him she couldn't fail to notice his glittering green, somewhat sleepy eyes.

Abiola became very frightened. For the first time she began to sense there was something wrong about her husband. He reminded her of something – exactly what she couldn't say.

'Why are you looking at me like that, my dear?' he asked Abiola who had also just noticed the strange, slightly scaly skin around his finger nails.

Abiola didn't reply. Without a word she suddenly hopped out of the carriage and began to run, holding up her wedding gown. In a flash her husband was after her. Abiola pushed and kicked him but he was stronger; he dragged her along with him to the little shack.

As soon as they reached inside, her husband began to undress himself slowly. As his fancy clothes fell to the ground she saw that he was nothing but a long, green-belly Camoudi.

Yes, how was the foolish girl to know that her fine gentleman-husband was none other than Camoudi snake who had heard all about the beautiful Abiola and decided he was going to try his luck with her. By some strange power Camoudi was able to change himself into a charming man by day, but when night caught up with him he turned right back into slimy green-belly Camoudi. Maybe if she hadn't been so swept away by Camoudi's charm, she would have noticed that look Tomo was warning her mother about.

Anyway, there was Abiola screaming for blue

murder and there was Camoudi coming towards
her smiling his horrible Camoudi smile and
singing:

> 'Ten, eleven men come to court you
> but you accept no one but me
> Ten, eleven men come to court you
> but you accept no one but me
> Me Camoudi, Me Camoudi . . .'

As he sang, he moved closer and closer, then
suddenly, with one sweep of his tail he encircled
her waist in a tight snake grip. Then he began to
swallow her slowly from her feet up.

Poor Abiola could do nothing much to save herself. She began to sing in a sad little voice, hoping
against hope that someone would hear her:

> 'Mammy-O, Pappy-O
> Camoudi a-swallow me
> Mammy-O, Pappy-O
> Camoudi a-swallow me.'

But Camoudi kept on swallowing. He was up to
her waist already and Abiola's voice was getting
fainter. She thought of Tomo and his lovely dark
eyes. She thought of her mother and father, all far
away.

Camoudi was now reaching her neck and
Abiola's voice was so faint you could hardly hear
it:

> 'Mammy-O, Pappy-O
> Camoudi a-swallow me
> Mammy-O, Pappy-O
> Camoudi a-swallow me.'

But just at that moment someone was bursting into the room with a loud noise. Someone was getting out his sharp fisherman's knife and slitting open the Camoudi's belly. Someone was pulling Abiola out and hugging her.

Yes, Tomo, the fisherman, who had always suspected Abiola's fine gentleman, had followed her all the way in his donkey-cart and was just in time to save her.

Two weeks later another wedding was taking place on the very sandy beach where Abiola and Tomo had first met. All the guests turned up again. And this time the birds sang in the clear blue sky as Abiola and Tomo danced under the shade of a palm tree. Everyone swore they made the happiest couple they had ever seen.

ANANCY AND MONKEY BUSINESS

(from Trinidad)

FAUSTIN CHARLES

ANANCY, THE cunning, trickster spider, was born in West Africa. A long, long time ago, he was caught and taken on a ship bound for the Caribbean.

Anancy was capable of turning himself into a man. He was the master trickster. He used tricks to get his own way every time, and he tricked even his own family and friends. That was how he lived, by trickery.

In the olden days, Monkey was not the mischievous, naughty, copy-cat creature that he is today; and he never lived in trees nor did he climb them. In those days he was the best dressed and best behaved animal in the land. He was a smooth talker with a sweet, gentle voice. He loved parading himself in a new suit every day, walking erect and proud, holding his head high in the air. Everyone loved and respected him, and called him '*Saga Boy** monkey'. The girls, especially, loved him and said he was the most handsome, the most charming creature in the whole world. As he came along the road strutting like a peacock, female

---

* *Saga boy*: a dandy who is loved by women

42

animals swooned, others cheered and clapped.

'I like the ground he walk on!' squawked a parrot to another.

'When he walk he so sure of himself!' sang a blackbird.

'Such a good-looking gentleman too!' cooed a dove.

'A master dresser!' said an armadillo.

Monkey was vain; he loved the praises that were showered on him; he smiled broadly and said, 'Thank you all. Good day to each of you.' Then he strutted elegantly on.

'Nobody can carry themself so well-mannered like him,' said a mongoose.

'He does never make a false step,' squeaked a squirrel; 'everything so right and proper.'

'I love Monkey so much!' hissed a snake. 'He nicer than a peacock.'

Anancy was leaning against a coconut tree, he saw and heard everything. He was very jealous and hated Monkey. He was thinking of a plan which would make Monkey into a laughing-stock, a joke in the eyes of everyone.

As soon as Monkey was out of earshot, Anancy shouted, 'All you can't see, Monkey is a show-off!'

'You talking nonsense, Anancy!' grunted a wild pig. 'You ain't in Monkey's class!'

'Anancy, you is a fool!' screeched some parakeets from a thicket of bamboo trees.

'Jealousy eating you up, Anancy!' said an opossum carrying her young ones on her back.

'Monkey don't do stupid things like you, Anancy!' shouted an agouti angrily from behind a silk-cotton tree.

'You always behaving crazy, Anancy!' said an ant-eater.

Anancy got very angry and said, 'All you is the ones who's crazy! I telling all of you that Monkey's mad. Tomorrow, come to this same place and all you going to see Monkey behaving crazy like a lunatic!'

The animals laughed at Anancy but promised to gather at the same place the next day.

'All you go see what a stupid clown Monkey is!' Anancy was fuming.

Anancy went and bought a lovely stylish jacket and made small holes in the lining. The next day he got lots of stinging ants and put them inside the lining of the jacket and waited for Monkey to pass by.

When Monkey appeared, Anancy went up to him and said very politely, 'Good day, Mr Monkey, sir.'

Monkey smiled and replied, 'Good morning to you, sir.'

Anancy grinned and said, 'Mr Monkey, I buy this jacket to wear to a wedding but I ain't know for sure if I should wear it. I don't know nothing about clothes. I know you have a great knowledge about clothes. I want you opinion about this jacket; tell me what you think about it.' Anancy was holding up the jacket to Monkey's face.

Monkey could not resist the temptation, his eyes were gleaming. 'Do you mind if I try it on?' he asked. 'Man, it so nice!'

'Yes, man, go on, put it on,' answered Anancy quickly. 'That's the best way for me to see it, on a great dresser like you.'

'Thank you,' said Monkey, taking off his jacket. 'Would you mind holding my jacket while I try on yours?'

'No, I ain't mind,' replied Anancy, smiling.

Monkey gave his jacket to Anancy and took Anancy's. He then put on Anancy's jacket, smiled broadly and said, 'There you are, how do I look?'

'You looking great, man!' exclaimed Anancy, 'but walk about in it, man.' Anancy began to walk towards the place where the animals were gathered. Monkey followed, walking stylishly.

The animals whistled! cooed! sang! cawed! grunted! growled! screeched! hissed! croaked! chirped! when they saw Monkey.

Then the stinging ants began to bite Monkey; he twisted and scratched, rolled his eyes and bit his lips.

'Shake you hand, Mr Monkey!' Anancy shouted at Monkey.

Monkey shook his hands about wildly.

'Jump up and down, Mr Monkey!' shouted Anancy.

Monkey jumped up and down, his face twisting and dripping with sweat, his whole body was shaking.

Then Anancy laughed loudly, and said, 'All you see! Monkey is a clown! He's a crazy fool! Look how he getting on!'

The animals were surprised and shocked, they could not believe their eyes.

Monkey was now rolling about on the ground, scratching, rubbing, groaning, kicking and moaning.

'Oh my,' hooted an owl, 'look at how Monkey getting on, like he mad. Anancy right, Monkey is a big joke.'

'Yes!' hissed a snake. 'Monkey was fooling us all the time. He's really a crazy fellar.'

'Everybody come and see!' yelled Anancy.

Animals came from all around, bewildered by what they saw.

'I woulda never believe it,' muttered a raccoon.

'It ain't Monkey,' croaked a bullfrog.

Monkey sprang up into a tree, swung from branch to branch, then ripped off all his clothes, chattering, 'The clothes biting me!'

'Go and take a bath!' Anancy shouted at Monkey.

Monkey scampered off to the river.

'I tell all you, Monkey is a idiot,' Anancy laughed. 'Now all you believe me?'

'Yes! We believe you, Anancy!' they all answered.

'Anancy, you is a very smart creature!' an owl hooted.

'Anancy is a wise spider!' grunted a wild pig. 'He was talking the truth all the time.'

'We must always listen carefully to what Anancy say!' squeaked a field-mouse.

'Who woulda thought that they would ever see Monkey prancing about like that, eh,' bleated a wild deer.

From that day, Monkey was looked upon as silly and mischievous. Everything he did was called 'Monkey Business'. He copied everyone, and was never taken seriously. And his favourite dwelling place was the trees.

THE GAULIN WIFE

(from the Bahamas)

PATRICIA GLINTON

ON A SOUTHERN Island, in a settlement at the edge of a lake where flamingoes nested, there lived a young man who was thought quite handsome by the local girls. This was an opinion he shared completely. Mothers with marriageable daughters fought to bake for him, cook for him, mend for him, pamper him and flatter him; in short, each was eager to do anything to ensure her daughter's place by his side before the altar.

For this winsome bachelor, Miss Lucy baked johnny-cakes several times a week. Miss Dora offered him *benne,** coconut and peanut cakes. Titty Missy plaited him a fancy hat of white pond top and brown coconut straw. Various other women supplied him with limeade on hot days and pear-leaf tea on cool days.

The daughters themselves, as you may well imagine, were not idle in the battle for this great prize. They fought to share his pew on Easter Sunday, to plait the maypole with him on Empire Day and to give him paper valentines.

---

* *benne*: type of sweet cake made from seed similar to sesame and sugar

48

Needless to say, the young man grew exceedingly conceited and cruel. He promised marriage several times a month to as many women. He went as far as the church door with two of them and abandoned them there without excuse or explanation. Many a girl he simply dismissed with some scornful phrase.

''E head too *picky*.* 'E *musse†* *bu'n‡* 'e hair out with too much lard an' hot comb.'

Another favourite, which was certain to embarrass the poor girl to whom it was addressed, went this way: 'What I wan' wit' dis big, hard foot gal; yuh could see she ain' use to nuttin' but runnin' over sea rock an' workin' fiel'.'

When he wished to be cruel, he was cruel indeed.

'De reason why 'e gat dem pop-out eyes is, 'e mother must have feel sorry for frog or goggle-eye fish.'

The girl to whom this particular salvo was fired was so vexed that she took to her bed for a week. Disgusted by his behaviour, his old granny who had raised him warned:

'Listen boy, you guh pick 'til yuh pick needle wit'out eye.'

One day, not long after, a woman and her daughter came to the settlement. No one knew where they had lived before. They did not belong to that Island and yet they had not travelled by the mail boat. (This piece of information was gleaned from Miss Lucy's husband who happened to be first mate.) This mysterious arrival caused a great deal of speculation. 'Dey musse come from Gaitor way.

---

* *picky*: short, sparse
† *musse*: must have
‡ *bu'n*: burn

Dem people so fool down dere, yuh dunno who
live dere.'

'No man, dey is town people. Yuh see dem lace
gown dey does wear?'

The ladies in question made no effort to satisfy
this curiosity, but rather whetted it. They never
left their house before sunset, they worked
no fields, they bought no fish, conch or crawfish
and they plaited no straw. How or what they ate
was no less puzzling than sea tides and Jack-o'-
lanterns.

There was, however, one fact that was known
by all – the daughter was extraordinarily beautiful.
It was not long before she caught the eye of the
young breaker-of-hearts. The courtship was not a
long one. It did not even run the course of the
hurricane season. The young man was welcomed
on the front porch during spring planting and he
married the girl when the first corn was harvested
in the summer. His granny died shortly before
the wedding. On her deathbed, she blessed her
grandson and said how glad she was that she was
'crossing the river' before he could make a fool of
himself.

If the grandmother had lived to see her 'child'
during the first months of his marriage, she would
have thought her judgement faulty for he was
extremely happy. This happiness, however, was
as fragile as the foam on the crest of a wave. By
the end of the first year, his wife's strange
habits, and lack of a child, made him thoroughly
miserable.

The cockiness which he had shown to the local
girls was gone. He had bragged to his friends that
he would have a son to carry on his name before
the new harvest. But the last ear of corn had been

picked, threshed and ground into grits and corn flour and there was still no boy; even a daughter would have allowed him to save some face.

Though he felt his failure to become a father keenly, this gentleman was even more troubled by the course of his wife's days. She and her mother (who continued to stay with them despite the husband's hints) rose before dawn, left the house and returned at sunset without excuse or explanation. No matter how he pleaded, cajoled, or threatened the pair, he could learn neither the direction they took, nor the reason for their wanderings.

After much thought, he decided that the matter was too great for his feeble, earthly efforts and so found himself in the presence of the local *obeah** woman upon whom he unburdened his woes. Mama Farida (for so she was called) directed him to bring to her a few strands of his wife's hair and some threads from a frequently worn dress. This he did.

Mama Farida filled a drinking glass with water and added to it the items which the young man had brought. From a pocket in her skirt, she pulled out a bag filled with shredded leaves and a brown powder. The exact composition of this pot-pourri was known only to Farida. A pinch of this mixture was added, then the glass was capped by a small mirror.

After these preparations, the obeah woman pulled a pipe from the aforementioned pocket, filled it with what was obviously dried bay geranium, sprinkled on a few grains of nutmeg, lit the mixture and inhaled deeply. Over and over again,

* *obeah*: witchcraft

between puffs, she spoke the words, 'Yanday, Yanday, turra day, oh!' She soon fell into a trance. She remained silent and motionless for so long a time that her visitor began to think her dead. When she did stir at last, she frightened him considerably by a burst of very loud singing in a voice that was obviously that of a man:

> 'When de pond, plonga, plonga,
> Meetee B'er sea crab, plonga, plonga
> Meetee B'er Gaulin, plonga, plonga.'

The water in the glass began to boil as if its container had been put upon a fire. The mirror upon it clouded over as mirrors do when breathed upon. Suddenly it cleared, revealing the image of a great ugly bird. The bird hovered for a moment in the mirrored sky, then swooped down to scoop up with its beak several crabs which scurried across a beach below. The whole scene vanished from the mirror when Mama Farida cried out, 'Poor fool, yuh married B'er* Gaulin.'†

By this time, if called upon to do so, the horrified client would have been unable to moisten his finger to test the direction of the wind. Mama Farida was forced to shake him from his stupor. From her bountiful pocket, she drew a length of string in which she tied seven knots. She looped it about the fellow's waist, under his shirt, with these words: 'I guh‡ help you 'cause yuh granny was muh frien'. Me an' her was mate, we born de same day. Now, boy, don' loose dis from yuh wais' 'til I tell yuh.'

---

* *B'er*: Brother
† *Gaulin* or *Gaulding*: a West Indian term for heron
‡ *guh*: will

After this, she described a procedure he was to
follow that night: 'When de gal an' 'e ma sleepin',
sprinkle salt round dey bed. Take dis bottle o' bay
rum what I guh gi'e yuh an' pour some on de two
a dem. But I done tell yuh, if yuh take off dem knot
from roun' yuh wais' 'fore yuh do this, dog guh be
better dan you.' She then advised him to run to
fetch her once he had completed these preparations.

Unfortunately, love has a way of bringing about
forgetfulness. When the young man looked upon
his beautiful wife again, he at once felt ashamed
of his suspicions. In secret, he cast away string
belt and bay rum, mumbling to himself, 'Dese ol'
woman – dem don' know what dey talkin' 'bout.
Farida better stop smokin' dem funny pipe.'

As the night wore on however, his doubts rose
like restless spirits to haunt him. Thus it was,
when wife and mother-in-law began their daily
journey, the husband followed secretly. The two
women walked quickly through Miss Lucy's to-
mato field which bordered the husband's property
and past a lime kiln which had burned for days
before but had been slaked by rain in the night.

They passed through glistening spider webs, dis-
turbed still-sleeping birds, crushed small land
crabs, to all of which they were oblivious in their
haste to reach their destination. The husband, still
pursuing, found that his curiosity increased with
the pace of the march, which, in turn, quickened
as the light grew. To the man following, it seemed
that the women had engaged in a furious race with
the sun. Faster and faster, brighter and brighter
until the sun and her rivals converged upon the
flamingo lake in an eerie dead heat.

The husband, as might be expected, ended his

journey just within the forest of the lake. There, he was to witness a spectacle, the like of which he had never seen in his life and which he was never to see again.

At first, the women stood motionless upon the sandy verge. Suddenly, the air was darkened by a flock of great ugly gauldings which swooped down to form a circle around the pair. To the astonishment of the watcher, the creatures tugged with their beaks at cloth, lace and fastenings until the human couple stood as bare as their grannies first saw them. What is more, the two showed no signs of alarm.

Without warning, the birds began to flap their wings frantically and sing in harsh human voices:

'When de pond, plonga, plonga,
Meetee B'er sea crab, plonga, plonga
Meetee B'er Gaulin, plonga, plonga.'

With the first words, the women began to scream dreadfully, as if in unbearable pain. Their necks stretched to twice the normal length, the cords standing out as taut as a bowline.

Their teeth and hair fell out as their lips protruded and hardened into beaks. Arms became wings, feet became talons and the screams continued to fill the air. When feathers had replaced soft brown skin, the transformation was complete. Where wife and mother-in-law had been, there were now two fierce gauldings.

Utter silence prevailed for the space of a heartbeat. Then the husband took up the screaming which his late relatives had only just left off. Thus discovering that their ritual had been observed, the strange birds rose into the air with deadly purpose.

They soon spied the maddened onlooker who was
now too witless to realize the need for continued
concealment. Enraged, they pecked at his eyes,
tore his clothing and finally rose into the air
clutching the unfortunate man in their talons.
Higher and faster they flew until the clouds
covered their flight. Their hapless victim was
never seen again. The people of the settlement
claimed that he had gone 'to foreign parts' with
his wife, which was, in large measure, true.

> *Biddy bo ben*
> *Go to where flamingoes fly*
> *And ask them to disprove this lie.*

THE ADVENTURES OF ROSE PETAL

(from Barbados)

MERLENE BRATHWAITE

MANY YEARS ago, no one knows quite how many, there lived, somewhere around the Caribbean Islands, a very beautiful girl, whose name was Rose Petal.

When Rose Petal was born, her mother looked outside the window and saw the rose petals falling from the trees. The rose petals looked lovely blowing in the gentle breeze and a handful of them blew in through the open window and settled gently on the baby's cradle. The baby opened her eyes and smiled. Her mother called her Rose Petal.

Rose Petal was only a child when her dear mother died, and her poor father, not being able to do the housework and look after the child, decided to marry again. Unfortunately, Rose Petal's father married a woman who was not only ugly, but wicked as well. This wicked woman had a daughter as ugly and as wicked as herself. As soon as Rose Petal was old enough, her stepmother and stepsister made her do all the housework. She had to do the washing, cleaning, the cooking and mending, the feeding of the animals and the spinning of the thread to make clothes. Whenever Rose Petal was sick, or if she was caught resting from overwork and tiredness, the wicked stepmother would give her a sound beating and the ugly stepsister would taunt and tease her. And so, Rose Petal lived a very miserable life.

One bright, sunshiny day, whilst Rose Petal was sitting peacefully by the river sewing some torn clothes, the sewing needle suddenly slipped out of her hands and fell softly into the water. 'Oh dear,' said Rose Petal, feeling very distressed. 'Whatever shall I do!' And she ran home as fast as she could to tell her stepmother. The stepmother was so angry that she boxed the girl's ears soundly and told her to return to the river at once and search for the needle, even if she had to jump into the water to find it.

Rose Petal returned to the riverside. She searched high and low but could not find the needle. Too afraid to go home without the needle, the poor girl decided to jump in the river to see if she might find it at the bottom on the river bed. She forgot that she couldn't swim.

As soon as Rose Petal jumped into the cool, blue water, she began to sink slowly down, down, past all manner of beautiful coloured fish, some stopping to observe the lovely stranger, some swimming briskly away to hide. It seemed as if she would never reach the bottom but, at last, she landed with a thump. When she opened her eyes, she found that she was in a beautiful land, a land so full of wonderfully different things that it soon made her heart light and happy just to be there. Rose Petal skipped through the meadows, admiring the green fields, the tall, elegant trees and the beautiful flowers of many colours dancing in the gentle breeze. The birds were happily chirping a beautiful melody, while the butterflies and the bees were busy flitting from one flower to another. All the animals were very friendly and followed Rose Petal everywhere. Soon Rose Petal was feeling very tired and slightly hungry, so the animals led her to a quiet, shady spot under a row of large trees, which were near the path. Rose Petal ate her fill of ripe red cherries and soft golden mangoes. She had never tasted so much delicious fruit in all her life. At her father's house there were fruit trees in the garden but Rose Petal had never been allowed to eat the fruit.

Soon Rose Petal fell into a long, peaceful sleep. When she awoke, the sun was going down behind the hills, and the bright, cheerful day had turned into a cool, calm evening. She found her way on to the path and had not walked very far when, by chance, she met a traveller, who told her of a cottage just beyond the trees, where a dear old lady lived who helped lost strangers. When Rose Petal reached the cottage, she knocked softly on the door. A friendly, white-haired old lady gently opened it. Her eyes were soft and warm and her voice was very pleasant. Rose Petal told the old lady (whose name was Mother Nature) all that had happened to her and that she was now lost. Mother Nature said that she would be happy to help the girl and she asked Rose Petal to stay a while with her and help her with the housework as she was getting too old to manage it on her own. Rose Petal answered that she would gladly stay and Mother Nature showed her to her room, which was a lovely shade of rose pink, with a large, fluffy bed in the middle and a wooden floor so beautifully polished you could see your face in it. Then Mother Nature took Rose Petal into another room, which was brilliant white all over, decorated with long,

lacy curtains, which shimmered and shone when they caught the light and the gentle breeze from the open window. Instead of a bed, the room was filled with large, soft, fluffy white pillows, which looked like clouds.

'Now, Rose Petal,' said Mother Nature, 'early each morning, you must come to this room and shake the pillows, for this is the room of "joy and gladness" and when you shake the pillows all the joy and gladness will flow outwards and fill the world with happiness and all the boys and girls will run and jump and play and they will be very happy.'

Rose Petal was very surprised but she agreed to stay with Mother Nature.

Bright and early each morning she went to the white room and shook the pillows. To her amazement, all kinds of brightly coloured flower petals, in a variety of shapes and sizes, flew out of the pillow-cases and floated through the open window. Immediately the walls of the room changed into huge mirrors and through the falling petals Rose Petal could see all the boys and girls in the world running out of their houses to hop, skip and jump and play in the morning sunshine. All of them laughing joyfully and trying to catch the beautiful petals that were falling all around them. It made Rose Petal feel very happy to know that she was helping to spread so much joy. She could not, however, find her father's house when she looked into the mirrors.

At last, one day Rose Petal went to Mother Nature and said, 'Dear Mother Nature, you have been so kind to me and I have been so happy here, but my father will be very sad if I do not return home.' Although Mother Nature loved the girl and wanted her to stay, she took Rose Petal outside and showed her a very long, winding path.

'You must follow this path,' she said, 'and do not leave it. When you come to the end of the path, you will see two gates: on the left is a very beautiful, golden gate and on the right is a dull, old iron gate. If you go through the iron gate you will receive a good reward, but the choice is yours!'

When Mother Nature had finished speaking, she kissed the girl and gave her a basket full of precious golden apples, fresh, purple sea grapes, ripe, red cherries and a plate of pumpkin pie. Rose Petal thanked Mother Nature and went on her way.

It was a very long road but Rose Petal stayed on the path that Mother Nature had shown her, stopping only to eat something nice from her basket.

At last she came to the end of the path, where she saw the two gates. The gate on the left was made of shining gold, which glittered and glistened in the hot, bright sunshine, and there were jewels of many colours all around it. It was very tempting indeed to go through that breath-takingly beautiful gate. However, Rose Petal remembered what Mother Nature had told her and she went right up to the dull, old iron gate and walked through without a second thought.

As soon as the girl walked through the gate, a dazzling ray of light shone all over her, a soft bundle of gold fell gently from the top of the iron gate and covered her until she shone as bright as the light. Rose Petal was now the most beautiful girl in the whole world, full of grace and elegance. Some of the gold had fallen into her basket, so now she had something wonderful and precious to give to her dear father.

Rose Petal did not have far to walk before she saw her father's house in the distance. When she reached the front gate, the old cock began to crow, 'Cocka-doo-doo-doo — Your golden girl has come home to you!'

Rose Petal's father ran out of the house and hugged and kissed his daughter. He had believed his daughter had drowned, and seeing her again made him the happiest man in the world.

The stepmother and daughter were very surprised to see Rose Petal. They had seen her jump into the river and when they did not see her come out of the water again they had fallen into each other's arms in joy. They had hated poor Rose Petal because she had a gentle nature and a kind heart. She was also very beautiful to look at.

The stepmother now pretended that she, too, was happy to see Rose Petal, but both mother and daughter hated her more than ever, especially now that she was even more beautiful.

Rose Petal told her story about her adventures. She told them of kind Mother Nature, the brilliant white room with the wall of mirrors, the flower petal children and the path leading to the iron and the golden gates. When Rose Petal had finished telling her story, the stepmother grew so jealous that she was determined her daughter should have the same fate. She sent the lazy, ugly girl to the river the very next day, even before the sun was awake, with a bundle of clothes to mend. The clumsy girl ran all the way to the riverside, stumbling as she went. When she reached the river, the girl threw the bundle of clothes on to the ground and dropped the needle into the water and immediately dived in after it.

But, unfortunately, the door to Mother Nature's

world was closed. It was the wrong time of the year! So the poor girl was carried away by the angry river to another strange and wonderful land, where she too had many adventures. But that is another story!

As for the wicked stepmother, when her daughter did not return to the house after many months had passed, she went to the riverside to search for her, but to her dismay the river had dried up. The poor, old stepmother wept with grief and in her sadness she returned to the house. No one could comfort her, except Rose Petal, and after many years, she grew to love Rose Petal as her own daughter.

As for Rose Petal, the kind-hearted girl used the gold in her basket to help the poor people of her country and she was loved by everyone.

Yes, she *did* return to Mother Nature's world for a visit, taking her old father and stepmother with her. But that too is another story.

MARISSA'S ADVENTURE

(from Bermuda)

KELLY BURTON

GRANNY GRANT and Uncle Lewis often talked of the great mysterious Bermuda Triangle which carried away so many people including Auntie Vernice. It seemed so strange that out there somewhere was a triangle of space that ate people, ships, aeroplanes and everything that came within its reach.

It was growing dark, and the more Marissa thought about the triangle, the more she became afraid. The tall, dark palm trees that bent their heads with the swaying wind looked like giant monsters against the dark purple sky. The beach which had been so full of life that day became silent and eerie. Marissa's only thought was to get home quickly before the crickets began to sing, and the sun, which was quickly sinking towards the sea in the distance, went completely out of sight. Fear made her quicken her steps until she broke out into a run, past Mr Joseph's shack lit by candle light, down the hill and around the bend which marked the place where the bus had overturned ten years ago. Only six more trees to pass, one, two, three; she was nearly past the fourth one when a strange sound made her stop

in her tracks. The sound seemed to be coming
from the undergrowth. She looked through
the dense undergrowth and saw what she
thought was a giant turtle. It seemed to be
beckoning to her. She shook her head from side to
side as if to shake the thought completely from
her mind. As quickly as the turtle had appeared,
it disappeared and Marissa was left wondering
whether she had imagined it all. She decided
that she had imagined it and continued to run
the few yards to her house.

For Marissa, her home was like a huge squat
box. It was considered very posh indeed for that
area. The surrounding houses were little more than
single-storeyed concrete boxes painted in pastel
hues of pinks and blues. Many didn't have the
conveniences that Marissa's did. It was a two-
storeyed house with a white slated pyramid roof.
It had been designed and built by Marissa's great
grandfather forty years ago and had withstood the
hurricane winds which had hit the islands twice
since. Inside, the space was divided up between a
tiny kitchen in one corner with the remaining
space serving as a dining-room and living-room
combined. There were two bedrooms on the first
floor, one which was inhabited by Marissa's grand-
parents and one which Marissa had shared with
her older sister Waveney until she had left for
England to live with their parents. The house faced
west and as a consequence had no protection from
the hot sun. In the afternoon, the only two rooms
which were comfortable were the kitchen down-
stairs and the bathroom which was next to
Marissa's bedroom. To the back of the house was
a yard where Granny Grant kept four chickens, a
pig, a goat, and an old shabby cat which had been

with the family for as long as Marissa could remember.

Granny was waiting by the window for Marissa to arrive. Her grandmother wore her hair in two long silvery braids and her eyes, once bright and sparkling, had become soft and milky with the mellowing of time. She was a welcome sight as Marissa climbed the veranda stairs to the door. Even the harsh words for being late felt warm and comforting after the long and dark trek home. Grandfather sat quietly dozing in a corner. Marissa sat down to a hearty supper of *plantain,** sweet potato and rock fish. She washed it down with some guava juice, and kissing Granny, made her way up the stairs to bed. As she lay in bed staring through the window at the stars in the sky, her mind ran back to the vision she had had on her way home. A strange feeling of tiredness came over her and suddenly, she found herself standing on a lonely beach.

It was daylight! The sun was beating down on the hot, white, soft sand. Marissa was afraid to take another step for fear of burning her feet. It was then that she realized she was standing on the beach in her nightdress – whatever would Granny say? As she looked around she was aware that this was a stretch of the island that she had never been to. It could only be the place that Granny and her friends said 'funny things' happen at.

The sea was calm and inviting especially as the sun was so hot. Marissa, as if in a dream, danced towards the edge of the beach; she stood there looking at the turquoise water and was mesmerized by the glittering reflection of the sun as it

* *plantain*: a vegetable similar to a banana

transformed the water into a sea of sparkling diamonds. Then she suddenly noticed that something
large and brown was swimming towards her in the
crystal clear water. What was it? Marissa wanted
to run but felt as if her feet were fixed to the
ground. The shape was coming closer and closer.
She narrowed her eyes and was soon able to dis-
tinguish a turtle.

Once the turtle had reached within five yards of
the beach, it popped its head out of the water and
began to speak to Marissa. 'Hey, Marissa, my child,
I want you to hop on to my back because I am
going to take you for a ride that you will never
forget.' Although Marissa was afraid, she was
compelled to follow the turtle's instructions. She
wasn't sure what made her go. Was it because she
had never heard a turtle talking before, or was it
because she sought the adventure that the trip
promised? On to his back she climbed. She was
surprised how stable, safe and secure she felt. Before she knew it, the turtle had turned around and
was heading at full speed out to sea. Marissa was
a little anxious; she wasn't a strong swimmer and
the turtle was beginning to dive under the water.
She closed her eyes tightly as she felt the warm
water creep up from her knees right up to her face,
until she was completely submerged.

She was surprised that she was able to breathe
so freely. She expected to be coughing and splutter-
ing. She opened her eyes very slowly at first, ex-
pecting to see very little, except the murky black
water of the deep-deep sea. She was pleasantly
surprised to see the beautiful and the amazing
colours of the varied fish as they swam by. The
striped pilot fish winked his eye as Marissa and
the turtle made full speed ahead. They seemed to

be travelling for ages. Marissa was beginning to get tired, so she struck the turtle's shell very hard, taking care not to slip off. The turtle came to a halt. Marissa was so startled, she fell back and found herself falling, falling down, deep into the water. The turtle swam past her, and came up beneath to rescue her from the fall. 'Now, look here, child, you must be patient, we nearly there and if we stop, we'll lose time. Just think of all those amazing things I am going to show you.' So Marissa climbed back on and off they went again but this time at a slower pace.

After a while Marissa noticed that the colour of the water was beginning to change. It was gradually becoming light pink in colour. She was also aware that their path was being blocked by large objects like huge tree trunks.

'What are they?' cried Marissa.

'Only seaweed, child!' cried the turtle.

'Where are we?' cried Marissa.

'We are in the north Atlantic ocean between the coast of Bermuda, Puerto Rico and Florida. We are in the Sargasso Sea.' As soon as he had spoken the words, there was a great bright white light which seemed to engulf and swallow everything around it.

'Turtle!' cried Marissa, 'I am frightened, please tell me what is happening!'

The turtle said nothing but continued on his journey.

'Stop, turtle, I want to go back!' cried Marissa.

'It's too late now, child, we nearly there. We just about to enter now.'

'Enter what?' cried Marissa.

'Why the Bermuda Triangle,' said the turtle with surprise.

Marissa could hardly believe her eyes, but there in front of her was an entire underwater world. There were huge towers, built as if they were made of shimmering gold. Houses were made of coral and shells. As Marissa and the turtle swam past the buildings, Marissa noticed a large scaly tentacle appear from behind one of the buildings.

'What was that, turtle?' asked Marissa.

'Oh, just a giant octopus. Did your Granny never tell you about the wonders of the Sargasso Sea?'

Marissa and the turtle soon reached a huge castle-like building. Here the turtle stopped and asked Marissa to dismount. As she did so, he disappeared and she was left standing at the foot of a long line of limestone steps. At the top of the steps was a huge cavern which appeared to be the entrance to the castle. Marissa began to climb, quickly at first but she soon grew weary as the steps seemed to go on forever. When she eventually reached the top, she sat down to regain her breath.

A young maiden appeared from behind the cavern wall. Marissa was awestruck by her beauty: the maiden's hair fell like long sea-vines over her shoulders and down to her waist. She stretched out her hand and reached for Marissa. Marissa, as if transfixed, placed her hand in the maiden's and was pulled as if by a great force into a large hall. As the maiden released her hand, Marissa was astonished to see that part of the maiden's body was that of a fish. As suddenly as she had appeared, the maiden disappeared and Marissa was left alone in the huge hall.

The room began to be filled with beautiful music like the sound of harps and chimes. She could hear voices approaching and before she could turn to run, she was surrounded by a crowd of people, mermaids and fairymaids. One face stood out from the crowd. Marissa shook her head as if in disbelief – it was Auntie Vernice! She embraced her aunt with open arms and both of them wept happily. Aunt Vernice welcomed Marissa and told her not to worry as she had arrived in paradise. Marissa wanted to know so much! What was Aunt Vernice doing there? Who were all of these strange people? Why were they dressed in costumes that she had seen in history books and, most important, who and what were the mermaids and fairymaids?

Aunt Vernice told Marissa to calm down, and that all would be explained in due course. They were then ushered by two mermaids to a large ante-room where a banquet was being prepared. Everybody took a place at the enormous dining table. There was food and drink for everyone. Everyone seemed remarkably happy. After the feast, the merriment continued with dancing and singing and party games. Marissa was beginning to enjoy herself. The party did not seem to be coming to an end. Marissa nudged Aunt Vernice and said, 'I am tired, I would like to go home.'

Aunt Vernice smiled and then laughed aloud, 'Sleep!' she exclaimed. 'We have no need of sleep here. In paradise, my child, we play and play and play all day, and the night too.'

With that a mermaid grabbed Aunt Vernice by the hand and the two of them danced away in a swirling mass.

Marissa began to despair. She sat down with her face held in her hands. Where on earth was the turtle who had brought her here? A young fairy-maid sat down beside her and was puzzled by the sad look on Marissa's face.

'Human child,' she said, 'why do you look so

sad? Everybody else who has come here has come with goodwill. Upon entering the Bermuda Triangle they have found much happiness in our underwater paradise and have resigned themselves to the fact that once here they may never return to the world they once knew. Many have been led to this part of the world seeking treasure from lost ships instead of which they have entered paradise. Many ships have stumbled upon the triangle by accident. Throughout the centuries we have grown in our community from lost ships who have stumbled across paradise. We have even had aircraft pilots join us. They have left behind family, loved ones and friends, but once they have accepted their fate they have enjoyed all the pleasures that paradise brings.'

She also told Marissa that she was brought to the triangle by her thoughts and it was the turtle who as the messenger of the triangle was sent to bring her there. Marissa thanked the fairymaid for answering some of her questions; however, she was still unhappy.

As she sat watching everybody dancing, her thoughts went back to Granny Grant and grandfather. She could see Granny Grant sitting on the rocking chair looking out towards the sea with tears rolling down her cheeks. Grandfather pacing up and down with his hands clasped tightly behind his back. She thought of standing on Hamilton Harbour watching the ships come in. She thought of her school building and the children sitting down having their lessons. She thought of sinking her feet into the curving pink sandy beaches backed by grey rock; the gentle rolling hills and the sand dunes, all surrounded by the turquoise sea.

Just these thoughts of familiar things made her get up and run. She ran through the two large halls to the entrance of the castle, hesitated for a moment, and then fled down the many steps. Once she had reached the bottom, she tried to retrace the route by which the turtle had brought her. She did this quite successfully and found herself back at the astonishing barrier of bright light. She tried to get through but found her way blocked as if by some invisible barrier. She angrily thought, 'If this is paradise why do they try to keep people here?'

All she wanted to do was scream. As she did so, she felt a hand upon her shoulder shaking her. She also thought she heard the familiar voice of Granny Grant, telling her to wake up. As she opened her eyes, she saw the soft watery eyes of Granny Grant staring straight back at her; her immediate reaction was to hug and kiss her Granny. Granny Grant said, 'You are awake at last, child. Welcome back to the real world, you must have been having a bad dream.'

'Dream!' exclaimed Marissa, smiling as she reached down and brushed the wet sand from her feet.

THE IBELLES* AND
THE LOST PATHS

(from Cuba)

PEDRO PÉREZ SARDUY

Translated by Jean Stubbs

THE FIELDS had been planted with cane, and the
sugar mills were ready for grinding. Harvest-
ing was about to start on the tobacco and coffee.
Then all the paths and roads of Cuba mysteriously
disappeared, swallowed up by thick grass and
forest.

To travel meant certain death, because Death –
Iku – lay in wait, guarding the vanished routes.
From one end of the island to the other, fear of Iku
meant that each home, each village, each town,
rich or poor, was like a prison. Its walls were
invisible but still very real. Anyone who tried to
leave and walk through them never came back.

People were cut off, locked in their own world.
They had no means of communicating, even when
they lived quite close to each other. There were
those from the coast who had been marooned in-
land and wept at the sound of the wind rushing
through the leaves like waves. Those who came
from the interior but lived by the coast sighed at
the sea rustling like trees. Hill and woodland folk
died by the sea, and sea folk died stranded in the

---

* *ibelles*: twins

countryside. Even white folks, who had never been in chains or been given the whip, looked out over the horizon and felt like slaves.

Life stood still and weighed heavily. Desires, dreams and hopes vanished along the lost paths. Hearts were stricken with grief, boredom and nostalgia. Yet there were still some rebellious spirits who refused to take the unknown danger seriously.

'Fools' talk,' they said. 'It's time to rebel against fate and conquer fear and death. It's time to break down those terrible barriers.'

They'd risk ill-fortune rather than continue the nightmare of being captive to that strange monotony. But not one of them ever returned.

Down in Vuelta Abajo was an abandoned coffee plantation. Its white owner, a restless, ambitious man, left in desperation one day on horseback. His only son went to look for him, with the overseer and a handful of loyal slaves. The son wore his crucifix. The black slaves had their special charms to protect them. They were all armed to the teeth. Yet they never came back either.

The lady of the house waited in vain. In the end, she died of sorrow and was buried by the last remaining slaves under a leafy mango tree. It was one of the mango and orange trees that had once lined the paths and groves of the estate. Now, fertile land was overrun with weeds, thicket and undergrowth.

Twenty years or more went by. Yet there was still, on that tumbledown estate, an old African couple whose names people could no longer remember. The couple had had twenty children, boys and girls. But each of the boys, as he reached manhood, had gone to his father and said:

'I'm leaving, father. Bird doesn't want to live in

cage.' And with that, he'd disappear into the bush like a snake.

'Ay, ay, ay . . . my son's going away,' his poor mother had sobbed over each one.

Then, old as she was, much too old to have children, she gave birth to male twins, to magical ibelles. She was overjoyed. The happiest fiesta for twenty years rang out on the plantation. Watching her twins sleeping in their rough shelter of palm and dry bark, she sang:

> 'Ye ye ye, lukende, yeye
> Yeye, lukende, yeye'

The ibelles were like two coffee beans in a pod, absolutely identical. The first-born was Taewo, and the other, Kainde. Each wore an ebony cross on a jet pearl necklace and from each of their chests shone a bright light. The light, the elders said, had come into the world with them. It was the divine mark of the great African god Obatala.

Their mother doted on these miraculous sons, and all the other women watched over them as if they were their own.

'They come from the sky, sent by the gods Oloddumare and Olorun,' some of the women said.

'They are princes, sons of the mighty Orisha Shango – strong among the strong, heir to Olofi, the Creator of life,' others insisted. 'They are the only children who will be cherished by Yansa, Lady of the Cemeteries.'

The twins were fed on delicious fruits and white pigeon, they were bathed in sweet-smelling herbs, their bodies were smoothed with coconut oil. Celebrations were held, and there was dancing and singing in their honour.

They grew up full of fun and mischief. They were alike and very close. And when they were as tall as the lime trees, they too went to their father and said the words their brothers had said before them.

'Babami, mo fa iadde.'

Their mother began to wail, and she was joined by all the other women who loved them so much.

'My ibelles!' she cried. 'Now my ibelles are going too! My ibelles are going to die . . .'

Then, suddenly, an extraordinary hundred-year-old woman, who could no longer see or stand up straight, rose tall. For an instant, new life seemed to race through her. Movement came back to her stiff arms, strength to her legs which had been useless. She stood proud and upright as she had in her youth. Her voice rang out with a freshness above the women's lament, and the wailing gave way to songs of joy.

Laughing and crying at the same time, the women beat palm leaves around two identical wooden dishes and danced in a circle – the dance for rejoicing over twins – as the ibelles went further and further into the forbidden scrub.

The obeah men, who talked with the gods and the dead, said all the roads and the paths had closed up because of a devil: Okurri Boroku. This cruel and unpredictable ogre lay in wait for every travel-ler. He would put them through a test and when they failed – as they were bound to – he would gobble them up.

For seven days the twins wandered through thick undergrowth that parted to let them pass, only to close tightly again behind them. And they slept seven peaceful nights, unharmed, under the shelter of cedars and flamboyants and trailing plants. The presence of ibelles was enough to keep away the three wicked spirits of the wood, Chichicate, Manuelita and Guao.

The twins marched on, under the open sky, across flat stony land, fragrant with esparto grass and red ebony. In the distance, they saw some hills, which they then climbed, and for the first time saw the sea.

They wandered in those hills for another seven days. Then one morning they came down, and there, in the hollow of a small valley, was Okurri Boroku. He stood between two huge piles of human bones and was a gigantic, horrible-looking old man. He had a square face divided into two colours: one half was death-white and the other blood-red. His mouth stretched from one ear to the other, and he had sharp, bared teeth the length of a hunting knife. Bunches of feathers and strings streamed wildly from his enormous shoulders.

He seemed to be fast asleep on his feet in the drowsy valley, and one of the twins – Taewo – slithered like a lizard through the thick grass, which everyone knows has powers to undo evil. Okurri Boroku half-opened his eyes, then closed them again. Seeing that the demon was making no real effort to come out of his doze, the other twin – Kainde – ventured closer, grabbed one of the bunches of feathers, and shook it hard.

'Come on, wake up!' shouted Kainde at the top of his voice.

'Muuhhh . . . muuhhh,' grumbled the old ogre, stretching and gradually coming round, and the valley echoed with the roar of his yawn.

Then he noticed the ibelle. 'What are you doing here, boy?' he exclaimed, surprised. 'Don't you know my law? Boy, look at my teeth! I must have been asleep for years. No one comes by here any more. It's years since I tasted human flesh! And I'm hungry. Boy, look at my teeth!'

'Make way,' the twin said sweetly. 'Let me pass.'

'Yes, but first you must play my guitar and make me dance till I drop. If your tune's good and I like it, and if you can play longer than I dance, then you can pass. If not . . . gluh, I'll eat you up! Look at my teeth, boy. That's my law.'

The devil stuck his claws into a kind of kangaroo pouch under his ribs, took out a guitar and gave it to the boy.

Kainde started to play:

> Dinguirin Dinguirin Dinguirin
> Dinguirin Dinguirin Dinguirin

And then he sang:

> 'Dea mamandea dea mamandelin
> Dea mamandea dea mamandelin'

And then he played:

> Dinguirin Dinguirin Dinguirin

'Aaahhhh!' said the devil, going red from top to toe, his ears growing longer. 'I like it, boy. We'll dance.' And he danced non-stop for two, three, four hours . . .

The twin's fingers were hurting and his arm was beginning to go numb.

'Taita, I'm thirsty,' he said at last. 'I can see a well over there by that bush. Please let me have a drink.'

'Go and drink,' replied the devil.

Kainde ran to where his brother was hidden and they quickly changed places without the devil seeing.

Then Taewo took up the guitar and continued strumming:

Dinguirin Dinguirin Dinguirin

Sparks were flying from the dreaded Okurri Boroku. He'd shudder to a halt, suddenly jump forwards roaring with contentment, then shoot back surprised and furious, as if dodging some unseen enemy rushing at him. He'd spin around on the spot, dancing like a flame, not suspecting that, after all those years of sleep, he might not be as strong as he used to be.

Hours later, the twin again asked: 'Taita, some water.'

'Drink, boy, but look at my teeth!'

This time, it was Kainde who came back, refreshed. But the devil showed no signs of being tired yet. He was shaking his noisy scales and moving his feathers and creating a terrible racket with the thunder of his bells and the crash of his dancing.

'Taita, some water.'

'Drink, my child. You won't be able to drink as much as I can dance. There's a river behind the well – drink the river, boy! But look at my teeth. While you play, the devil will dance.'

Okurri Boroku was really enjoying himself. Fire kept shooting from his bulging eyes, from his huge mouth and his wobbly nose. Magnificent feathered flames darted from his tail. And, while the ibelle went off, pretending it was for a drink, he carried on dancing and burning, singing to himself:

Dinguirin Dinguirin Dinguirin

Then came Taewo, who'd meanwhile had a nap and devoured six of the twelve pigeons brought to him by a hawk.

The sun set, and it went dark. Another four hours passed while the ibelle strummed the guitar. The moon came out. Night birds flew down to dance with the devil in shadowy flocks around his hairy head. The heaps of bones cracked to life and the valley was filled with their silvery shapes roaming in all directions, chasing and bumping into each other. And Okurri Boroku swayed about, gasping for breath and delirious.

'Hey, Taita, I'm going to get a drink!' And the twin who took up the guitar watched him begin to spin again, reeling until at last he fell over completely.

'While I play, the devil must dance,' said the ibelle. 'This is your law! Taita, show me your teeth!'

The devil forced a smile, to show his large teeth. It was more of a horrible grimace, and wearily, he began to dance again. But he couldn't keep his body going. The fire had gone from his eyes. He was panting, his forked tongue hanging out. The twin made him keep going in time to the music. As owls and bats circled slowly around him, the devil teetered and lost his balance.

It was midnight in the blue valley covered in human bones.

'The water must be well chilled under the full moon,' said the ibelle.

Okurri Boroku had had enough. Tamed, beaten, he couldn't wait for the twin to stop playing even for a few moments. His body felt dead from the waist down, half-dead from the waist up. Without realizing it, he fell on his back, face up to the moon.

Dinguirin Dinguirin Din . . . gui . . . rin . . .

Very far away, he heard the guitar laughing . . .

'Your time has come!' the ibelles both said at the same time, as the ebony crosses on their necklaces spoke:

'Find three irons in the forest, a mallow plant and a clay pot. Tear out his heart, cut it in pieces, crush it with the leaves and bury it deep inside the pot.'

This the twins did, and it was the end of Okurri Boroku. The island was freed from the curse, and the paths began to appear again. The ibelles also brought back all those who had been lost. That very same night, they climbed up the Royal Palm, high into the sky, and asked Obatala, who never denied them anything, to return the bodies and souls to the thousands of skeletons left unburied in the valley and along the paths Okurri Boroku had blocked.

That was a long, long time ago, but in Cuba ibelles are still very special.

THE COQUÍ* AND GABRIEL

(from Puerto Rico)

ALFREDO ARANGO FRANCO

Translated by Blanca Vázquez

THIS STORY took place on the island of Puerto Rico. It was late one afternoon and powerful winds warned of an impending hurricane. A coquí who lived on the top of a plantain tree slowly descended the trunk looking for a nice humid spot where he could sing a song. As he jumped from place to place in the malojillo, which is a wild grass, he searched for a strong and tall plant. He wanted the other coquís and the crickets to be able to hear him when they sang to the night of the island.

On his left he saw a beautiful plant. He jumped on its branches but the sensitive moriviví, feeling his weight, began to close its leaves as soon as he landed. The coquí did not want to bother the plant so he jumped to the ground. Then he saw another plant and prepared to leap on it. This one was a thistle and its prickly thorns stung his stomach. He was uncomfortable and had to leave this plant too. Finally, a little further ahead, he saw a strong, large plant with flat, wide leaves called elephant's ears, ideal for a singer of his calibre. He jumped,

---

* *coquí*: a frog

85

gracefully falling on one of the beautiful green leaves. He found it to be a perfect place to spend a few hours practising his art.

He stretched out his arms and legs and felt relieved to have found what he was seeking. He thought about the other coquís and the crickets who were probably still looking for a good leaf on which to sit and sing. He had to give them a little bit more time; he didn't want to start singing ahead of the others.

He looked up at the sky and was surprised to see that there was not even one star. It was the first time this had ever happened. All his life he had found millions of brilliant stars that entertained him with their twinkling. He searched all over for the moon which is the loyal companion of coquís and could not find it. Then he realized that there had been no sunset that afternoon: it had gotten dark early and the night was very black. He sat there, thinking, and tried to understand what the darkening clouds could mean. At that moment, the wind picked up and shook the elephant's ear where he was sitting. He had to hold on fiercely with his little fingers and toes to keep from being flung into the air.

When the gust of wind had passed, he realized that it was late and no one had started to sing. Perhaps, as had happened before, everyone was waiting for someone else to start. Since he was well situated and in good spirits, he would begin. He rubbed his hands and stretched his neck, warmed up his throat and let out the sound for which coquís are named: 'coquí-coquí!' No one, neither the coquís, nor the crickets, cicadas, or birds answered his call. 'Coquí-coquí!' he called more loudly, but only the howling of the wind reached across the silence of the forest.

'This is very strange,' he said to himself. 'I have to find out what is happening.' With this in mind, he leapt from his comfortable leaf to the ground and began to look for someone. He stopped and cocked his ear trying to hear the sound of water. Coquís love fresh water and he was sure to find his friends there. But it was not to be. After a time he heard rumbling sounds coming from a ravine and quickly followed the sound, but found the place desolate. 'Perhaps on the other side of the creek,' he thought, and jumping from rock to rock he crossed to the other side. He searched and searched but found no trace of any living creature except plants, vines and shrubs.

He decided to solve this mystery. He found himself in a spot without trees and plants, a place with rocks and sand. He heard the roar of the seas; as he got closer and closer the sound was deafening. He had never heard the sea so angry before, and for a moment he was fearful, but he kept on going . . .

When he reached the beach it started to rain. The drops were heavy. The fierce wind blew up a sandstorm. Giant waves pounded the beach warning of the flood to come. Fearing for his life, he sought refuge behind some large rocks he distinguished in the darkness. Suddenly the rocks were heaved up by the force of the winds and a huge wave lashed at him. Hanging on to a rock like a tick, he thought his days were numbered. The hurricane was fully awake now. Before another wave could rob him of all his strength, he jumped to the highest rocks which formed the base of a great wall.

The water continued pounding and rising, higher and higher. To keep from drowning he climbed up the side of the rocks clinging to the ridges with all his might. He thought he would never reach the top. The further he climbed the more he felt the powerful winds that seemed to be pulling him from the walls with mighty hands. Fixing his gaze on the sky above, he kept on climbing until, trembling, he reached the top. Instinctively, he began to climb down the other side of the wall. The descent was as difficult, if not more so, than the ascent. When he finally touched the ground, he looked around for some place to hide from the furious rain. He had landed in a big patio, surrounded by heavy doors. It was the first time he had ever been in a man-made building and this confused him even more. He decided to go to the nearest door. Flattening himself, he squeezed under the door. He had hardly poked his wet face through when a foul odour hit him, as if the sun and fresh air had never entered this place.

On the walls were torches that barely lit the narrow passages. He hurried along one of the passages but halfway down he heard footsteps approaching. He squeezed against the wall and held his breath. At that very moment he saw a cockroach scurrying along the opposite side of the wall. For some reason, perhaps stupefied by the filthy odour, the cockroach did not seem to hear the footsteps. The coquí wanted to warn her but it was too late: the man was right in front of them. He had on heavy boots that stretched above his knees, short, wide breeches, a dirty shirt and a suit of armour that covered his chest and back. On his head he wore a brimmed iron helmet with some broken, greasy feathers on top. There was a heavy sword strapped at his waist and he carried a torch in his hand. His smell was repugnant. The cockroach now saw the danger and wanted to flee, but the man was faster and with a cackle lifted his leg for the squash. The coquí shut his eyes but he could not help hearing the horrible crunching sound of the roach under the man's boot.

The man spat against the wall and continued walking down the passageway. Without glancing back, the coquí hurried on along that dangerous corridor. He travelled down others no less frightening than the first, and heard the squeals of various rats. And since coquís and rats are not the best of friends, he decided that he'd better get out of there as fast as he could, having remembered the route so that he could find his way back. He jumped along passageways that were so dirty he could hardly breathe. Suddenly, he heard such sad moans that his little heart grew smaller inside his chest. Who could be in such a scary place and why did they moan in such a mournful way?

He moved closer to the sound to find out, and came upon a number of cells with iron bars. The sounds he had heard came from one of them. Inside the cell he saw something lying on the floor. He jumped in between the bars to see what it was. In spite of the darkness – only a dim light from a torch across the cavern reached the cell – he understood: it was a man, a black man, naked and covered with blood.

When the man noticed that the coquí was looking at him he stopped moaning and smiled. The coquí got closer and the man timidly stretched out his finger to touch him. The coquí put his little hand on the man's finger. The man spoke to him but the coquí did not understand, he did not speak the language of men. The man, who was suffering terribly, sat up, and with his knees drawn close into his chest, began to tremble and tell him incomprehensible things. He had manacles on his hands and ankles, and when he got agitated, the chains made a clanking noise that reverberated throughout. He became pale, and as he shook he began to get smaller and smaller. The coquí had seen the chameleon change colours, lightning bugs brighten the night as if they were distant stars, worms turn into beautiful butterflies who flew whimsically from flower to flower, so that he was not surprised when the man got smaller and smaller and began to change his form until he became a little green frog just like himself. The chains fell around him. The man-frog said, 'My name is Gabriel. What is your name?'

'Coquí,' answered the coquí. 'Why are you imprisoned here in this deplorable condition?'

'These men tore me and my parents from our land, gave us other names, and made us slaves. I am here because I escaped from a sugar plantation. The hunting dogs and the overseer found me and tortured me. Later my master turned me in to the authorities. He was afraid the other slaves would follow my example. Right now, in a boat in the bay, is a skilled executioner who comes from Cartagena de Indias where slaves are also escaping. They are keeping me here until he disembarks so that he can kill me in front of all the people. I don't know what they are waiting for.'

'A great hurricane has hit the island,' answered the coquí. 'How is it that you can change into a frog like me?'

'I learned how to do that from my wise ancestors in Africa. Their magic is very powerful, but if I

knew more I would not be here with my bones
broken.'

'Your magic is enough to escape from here. In
this form you can escape without being seen.'

'I can't stop my pain by changing my shape. I
can't move well. Anyway, I don't know the way
out of here. I would get lost. This fortress is so big
that even the men who built it get lost, and I would
be eaten by a rat if I tried.'

'Not if I help you. If you feel well enough I can
carry you on my back. I memorized the way in and
I'm sure I can find my way out,' answered the
coquí.

'Can you carry me?' asked Gabriel.

'Of course I can. I am a very strong coquí. Either
we both get out or neither of us will. Only, we
should wait at least three days until the hurricane
calms down.'

The coquí and Gabriel waited at first in a corner
of another cell. Nothing happened the first day.
They passed the hours quietly while Gabriel told
the coquí about the beauty and the mysteries of
Africa. On the second day, three rats suddenly
appeared. Driven crazy with hunger, they rushed
towards Gabriel and the coquí to bite them. Without wasting a second the coquí threw the man-frog
on his back and leapt so high into the air that the
confused rats could not see where they landed.
From this experience they both learned that the
slightest distraction could cost them their lives.
They stayed alert so as not to be surprised like that
again.

The third day of waiting was awful. The guards
discovered that the slave was not in his cell. They
couldn't understand how he could have escaped.
The gate was still locked. How could he move after

the beating they had given him? They searched all over for him. The captain ordered that the entire fortress be searched. Passageways, cells, sleeping quarters, and workrooms were filled with heavy boots stomping everywhere and swords poking into every corner. The coquí and the man-frog had to move quickly from hiding place to hiding place. It was dangerous to stay in one place too long.

When the soldiers found that the search was useless, they brought ferocious dogs into the gaol. With their sticky noses to the floor, the dogs smelled every inch of the place. When they sniffed something, the lighted torches were thrust where the beasts could not reach. That was the worst. They were in danger of being burned alive. The coquí found the most humid places to hide where the water could protect them from the flames, but the drain pipes filled by the water of the hurricane were also dangerous.

As they passed a room that had a strange odour, Gabriel said, 'This is the room where they store the gunpowder. They wouldn't dare bring the torches in here because they'd blow themselves up into little pieces. Let's hide here.' And so they did. They slid under the door and hid behind some big iron cannon balls where they spent the third day.

When the coquí and the man-frog came out of their hiding place, they made their way out of the cavern, and found themselves in the big patio surrounded by the high rock wall. The patio was filled with many soldiers and people in tattered clothes, exhausted and crying. The hurricane had destroyed their homes. Among them Gabriel saw the master who had put him in chains and turned him over to the soldiers to murder him. At the

wall, Gabriel said to the coquí, 'I feel much better.
You don't have to carry me on your back. I want
to climb the wall myself.'

The coquí and the man-frog climbed the wall
with a lot of difficulty and climbed down the other
side until they reached the rocks. It was a sunny
day. A clean breeze filled the air. The sea was calm,
and the white foam barely touched the beach. The
boat in which the executioner waited in vain for
his victim was now no more than little pieces
floating on the water: the hurricane had destroyed
it as if it were a toy.

Gabriel looked back pensively at the wall. Leaping away from it, they made for the dense forest.
The plants were greener, the flowers were a more
brilliant red, white and yellow. Everywhere, there
were bananas, mangoes, oranges, pineapples, and
fruits of all kinds.

Once they reached the malojillo, after crossing
the creek, Gabriel stopped and said, 'I never
thought that coquís were so brave. Now I have to
go. There are others who need me. You have helped
me tremendously, and we shall always be brothers.
What can I do to show you my gratitude?'

'You have shown me many things; I had never
spoken with a man. If you want to do something
for me, show me the most valuable thing you
know,' said the coquí.

'The most valuable thing I know is that we must
not let ourselves be turned from our lands and
enslaved, but must fight until death if necessary.'

Gabriel said goodbye and turned into a man
again. He took to the road in one direction while
the coquí took to the other, leaping from place to
place, looking for his house in the plantain tree so
that he could rest. He wanted to be wide awake and

alert that night. He slept profoundly and dreamt of all the beautiful things he had heard about Africa from his brother Gabriel.

That night, the coquí left his house and climbed down the plantain tree looking for a good place to start singing his story. From a very comfortable leaf he began his song and when he finished, thousands of coquís who heard him repeated the song for all coquís to hear, all over the island. It is a song that will never be forgotten by future generations of coquís. From that moment on, all the coquís fiercely resolved that they would not live in any place other than Puerto Rico, and for that reason, when they are taken to any other land, they prefer to die.

MAICHACK

(from Venezuela)

SORAYA BERMEJO

M AICHACK was so lazy . . . He was the laziest boy in the whole tribe, so his friends said. Things got to a point where the people of Camarata, Maichack's town, had to kick him out of the tribe. And they were so angry with him, so very angry that they chased him into the jungle. He ran, and ran, and ran until he found a good place to hide. As night approached, Maichack watched the animals heading for home and getting ready for supper. Maichack was hungry; so very, very hungry. He thought of his parents and sisters, and wondered what they were having for supper that night. And, since Maichack was lazy but not stupid, he took a *chile** and a piece of *casabe*† out of his pocket (he had taken them from his grandma's kitchen in advance, just in case, you know) ate half of them, and decided to use what was left as a kind of very personal alarm system.

He placed a piece of casabe and a bit of chile

---

* *chile*: chilli
† *casabe*: a kind of Indian bread made from yucca, an edible root

on the lowest branch of a nearby plant, and told them:

'You two are going to tell me when those people who came after me are approaching.'

He then walked a little further, and placed another piece of casabe, another bit of chile on a nearby plant, and said once again:

'You two are going to tell me when those people who came after me are approaching.'

He had walked for half a mile when he heard the casabe screaming. A bird had taken it, but Maichack said to himself:

'The people are coming!'

He started to run wildly until he suddenly realized that he was in a part of the jungle he had never seen before. He was lost. Then he saw a *curiara** moored to the river bank, and jumped into it, sadly realizing all of a sudden that he had been too lazy to learn how to paddle. A bird sang to Maichack: 'Tie a rope to the curiara, and I'll pull you up the river!'

Maichack saw no objection to the bird solving the problem for him, so he accepted. Soon, he was peacefully asleep on the curiara. For twelve days and twelve nights, the bird pulled the curiara up the river, until it got tired of doing all the work, and with Maichack still asleep, it tied the rope to a tree and left. When Maichack woke up, he found himself alone, and he was as lost as he had been before meeting the bird. He took a look around the place. It was the source of the river, peaceful and quiet. Thinking that it was a nice place to live in, a place where nobody would call him lazy, and tell him what to

* *curiara*: a long canoe

do, Maichack planted a *conuco** and decided to stay.

Soon he made friends with Pisimá, a being half man, half beast, who is invisible to all Indians except to the *piaches.*† Pisimá taught Maichack all kinds of things and, in no time at all, the boy became very adept. If we judge by the high standards of Maichack's fellow tribesmen, he was still quite lazy, but since there was nobody there to do the work for him – certainly not the great Pisimá – he had to work whether he liked it or not.

Maichack learned how to make casabe out of the yucca he had planted in his conuco. He also learned how to make tools, and when he got tired of eating casabe, he decided to try his luck at hunting. To his delight, he caught a deer. As he was eating it (a whole deer wasn't much for an appetite like Maichack's) he started to think about his lonely existence in the middle of the jungle, and how nice it would be to have a friend to chat with. Pisimá, though a good teacher, wasn't much of a talker. 'A friend would make all the difference,' he thought. And he wiped away a few tears, which he attributed to a bit of indigestion. 'It was rather a big deer,' he said to himself. But we know better.

Since a human friend was unlikely to be found in such a deserted part of the jungle, Maichack decided to settle for an animal one.

'I'm going to catch a *zamuro*‡ king to keep me company.'

So he put some tapir fat all over his body, and once he was all nice and sticky, Maichack let the

---

* *conuco*: a patch of ground used by the nomadic Indians to plant a few vegetables for their daily needs
† *piache*: witch doctor
‡ *zamuro*: a bird (carrion vulture)

fat decompose, and lay down on the floor playing dead. Soon, the zamuros arrived with the clear intention of eating Maichack. But just as he had planned, Maichack caught a zamuro by the neck, and took it home with him. Despite the rough start, they got to be good friends.

But there was something mysterious going on in Maichack's hut. Every single day, Maichack went hunting before dawn and came back long after dusk, and every single day he found his hut clean and tidy, and a delicious hot dinner waiting for him. However, there was nobody there but the zamuro.

One night, Maichack mentioned casually, as if talking to himself, that the next day he would come back later than usual. But the next morning, instead of going hunting, Maichack hid behind some bushes near his hut, and waited until midday. He then entered his hut, and found a beautiful woman cooking casabe, *cachirí,* * and some other of his favourite dishes.

'Where did you appear from?' Maichack asked her.

'I am the zamuro princess,' said the woman, 'and I live here with you.'

Well, Maichack wasn't one to argue with a good cook – particularly when she was the zamuro princess. So life went on as usual for a long, long time. Until one day, the zamuro princess got homesick and told Maichack:

'I would like to visit my father, the zamuro king. Let's go to his palace.'

So they got on the curiara, and went down the river. They travelled for twelve days and twelve nights, until they reached the palace of the zamuro

* *cachirí:* a jungle animal, similar to a small pig

king. Once at the door, the zamuro princess said
to Maichack:

'Wait here, Maichack; I'm going to ask my father
whether he wishes to see you.'

This was a sound and wise procedure, for when
people came to see the zamuro king he used to eat
them up in most instances. So the zamuro princess
announced to her father:

'There is a man out there called Maichack; he
would like to see you.'

'Very well, my daughter,' said the zamuro king.
'Let's see what kind of man he is.'

The zamuro princess led Maichack to the throne
room. It was very dark. Maichack could hear the
zamuro king's voice, but he could not see his face.
As soon as he heard them enter, the zamuro king
growled:

'If you are a good worker, Maichack, you may
stay; if you are not, I'll eat you up!'

And to test Maichack, the zamuro king ordered
him to drain an entire lake. The job had to be done
in one single day, and Maichack was also to catch
as many fish as he could for the zamuro king's
dinner.

Maichack went to the lake, not knowing what
to do. A dragon-fly circled by and asked:

'Why are you so sad, Maichack?'

'I am sad because I can't find a way to drain this
entire lake within one day, and if I don't do it, the
zamuro king will eat me up.'

'Don't worry,' the dragon-fly said. 'I'll help you
out.'

And, suddenly, out of nowhere, a dark cloud
covered the sky above the lake; millions of
dragon-flies had come to help Maichack drain the
lake.

Then, a bird called Oimi appeared and told Maichack:

'I will sing to let you know when the zamuro princess is coming. She shouldn't know that the dragon-flies are doing the work for you.'

And so Oimi kept watch at a short distance, and whenever the zamuro princess came to check how the work was coming along, the bird let Maichack know, and all she got to see was her poor friend looking very tired, very lonely and working, working, working. The dragon-flies emptied the lake by mid-afternoon. And Maichack, very proudly, presented the zamuro king with a hundred baskets of fish.

The next day, the zamuro king said to his daughter,

'My dear child, Maichack appears to be a very hard-working man. We will test him for three days, and if he comes out of it successfully, you can marry him if you wish. If he does not succeed, however, I will eat him up. His next task will be to build me a house, right there, on top of the big round rock.'

Maichack went to take a look at the place. It was just that: a BIG, round, hard rock. There was no way he could set the four poles for the house on that! He threw himself to the ground, and started to cry.

'I will not get out of this one! If only Pisimá, my old master, was here, I'm sure he would know what to do!'

No sooner had he mentioned Pisimá's name than a very tiny worm appeared right in front of his eyes. The worm told Maichack:

'Don't worry, I'll drill four holes in the rock, and you can use them to set the poles.'

Maichack started to laugh.

'You are such a small creature! I'd really like to see you do that . . . Oh, never mind, at least you have made me laugh, and forget my sad future as the zamuro king's main course. I'd really like to see you do that!'

Maichack laughed louder and louder, and the worm, who for a worm, had an excellent sense of humour, also started to laugh. But suddenly, Maichack grew silent. The worm was growing! It kept laughing louder and louder, and the louder it laughed, the bigger it grew. Well, as soon as the worm stopped laughing, it was a matter of minutes for him to drill the holes in the rock. And with the help of the animals from the jungle who collected the materials, built the wooden floor, the walls, and the palm roof, Maichack had the house ready in no time at all.

The zamuro king was very pleased with it. So pleased in fact, that he decided he needed a new throne for his new house.

'It will have to be very big, be able to walk by itself, and look just like me.'

And, guess who was going to build it? Well, Maichack, of course. After all, he had proved to be such an ingenious, industrious and clever fellow, that making a throne would be nothing compared to what he had already achieved. But let alone the fact that the throne had to walk by itself, there was a tiny, tiny problem. Nobody knew what the zamuro king looked like! It was rumoured that he had two heads, but he always managed to hide them from those who came to visit him. Maichack, nevertheless, started to make the throne, hoping that something would turn up. And so it did. For mind you, Maichack wasn't half as lazy as he was lucky.

A termite saw what he was doing and said:

'What are you doing, Maichack?'

'I am trying to make a throne that must resemble the zamuro king, but I am in trouble, for he has never let me, or anyone else, see his face.'

'I know exactly what to do,' said the termite. And he sent his friend *Tucusito** to take a look at the zamuro king's face. Tucusito could fly so fast, that he could go anywhere unnoticed. So he entered the palace and flew around the zamuro king once, and then again, but he just couldn't see his face. It was too dark. Tucusito, however, wasn't going to let such a small inconvenience get him down. He called his friend *Turpial*,† and asked him to sing under the zamuro king's window. It sang so beautifully! The zamuro king just couldn't resist the desire to draw the curtains back, open the window and see who the singer was. The room was immediately filled with light, and Tucusito was able to see that the zamuro king did indeed have two heads, and that he wore earrings. And so the two birds flew to tell Maichack and he asked the *comején*‡ to carve the throne. It was ready by midday.

Maichack took the throne to the zamuro king and his daughter. The king said, 'It bears a slight resemblance.'

To Maichack and everybody else's surprise the throne answered back: 'I am your very image.' And it approached the zamuro king walking just like a dog would. This did not surprise Maichack, for he

* *Tucusito*: humming bird
† *Turpial*: troupial, a bird
‡ *comején*: termite

knew that the throne was full of termites, and it was they who made it walk (and, probably, also talk) but it frightened the zamuro king to death. He screamed and ran out of the room. After he had calmed down, he said, 'Maichack you have done well! You frightened me, but you have proved to me that you are a good worker. You can stay, if you please, and marry the zamuro princess. I'm getting old. I'm tired. Soon the kingdom of the zamuros will be in need of a young and wise king. My daughter and you shall inherit my kingdom.'

Maichack was so proud of himself! All the zamuros of the jungle wanted to congratulate him, and they started to fly above Maichack and his bride, as a tribute to their future king and queen. Maichack felt then a strong desire to fly. 'But humans cannot fly,' he thought. 'Oh, if I could just . . .' Maichack closed his eyes. He thought of his old friend, Pisimá, and all of a sudden his body became very light, as light as the air of the jungle.

Maichack could fly.

THE ELF-STONE

(from the Dominican Republic)

JEAN POPEAU

JUANITA longed to marry Roderigo, a rich man living in Santiago, a town in the north of the Dominican Republic. She was from a nearby village and she had had a hard life full of misfortune and sorrow. She had come to town to seek her fortune ten years ago. If she married this man, she might gain some happiness at last, she thought. She deserved it! They were now going out with each other regularly, but she knew she was not his only 'girl friend'.

She went to consult a 'love expert' on the edge of town, that is, an old woman who knew all the secret ways to win a man's heart, and persuade him to marry you.

The old woman's head was tied in a large red-and-black striped scarf and she wore a bright blue dress which covered her feet. She was puffing slowly from a long pipe. She drew the curtains and enveloped the room in gloom.

'What is troubling you, my child?' she asked Juanita between puffs.

'I want to marry a man,' said Juanita.

'Don't we all,' said the old woman. 'Even I have hopes . . .'

'He's a rich man,' said Juanita simply.

'Any man will do for me,' said the old woman, 'as long as he's not too old, and not too stupid.'

'I am a poor girl. I have nothing – although some people say I'm beautiful. I want to know how to win him.' Juanita said this very simply and boldly.

'Well, I see you know what you want. I like a woman who knows what she wants. Too many of us are so silly. We marry a man "for love", when we could marry for other things – like money.' The old woman was equally candid with Juanita.

'Oh, but I do love him. He makes my heart weak every time he comes riding by on his tall black horse. But I have had to work hard all my life. I would like to lead a different kind of life when I marry. If I marry Roderigo, at least my life will change.'

'Yes, your life will change and you will become rich! Marry him for his money: love can always come afterwards! But you know, what you propose is difficult. A rich man must have many women after him. You must get an elf-stone.'

'An elf-stone?'

'Yes, with an elf-stone I can call the man you love. The charm of the stone works only in the afternoon, and you need a picture of the man.'

'I have a picture of him here.' Juanita showed her the picture.

'I will keep that. Yes, a handsome devil. He does not look too stupid ... I will put the picture under the elf-stone and lay it on the ground at a crossroads when the rain is falling and the sun is shining at the same time. I will point it in the direction the man usually comes riding from. I won't speak until the rain is over. Then I will bury the picture three feet underground and take the stone away with me.'

'What is your price?' Juanita asked solemnly.

'I want ten thousand pesos when you marry your man.'

'What, ten thousand?'

'That's my fee. I'm a poor woman too.'

'All right, I will pay you, after I'm married.'

The old woman told Juanita she would have to get the elf-stone from the mouth of a grotto, or small cave, in the forest, ten miles from Santiago.

'Who are you going to take along with you?' asked the old woman.

'My brother.'

'No, you must not take a man with you. You will not be able to get the elf-stone. If a man approaches near the pool, the elves will not allow you to take the elf-stone. I will come with you: I haven't seen an elf-stone for some time. I have nothing else to do.'

'When shall we go?' asked Juanita.

'I'll meet you at half past four outside the cemetery gate,' said the old woman.

'You think we'll need protection for the journey? It must be a dangerous road.'

'Don't worry, I will bring something to protect us.'

Later when they met outside the gate of the cemetery at the back of the church, the old woman had a small cloth bag in her left hand; a large *cutlass** glinted in her right hand.

'This is for our protection,' said the old woman, 'in case we meet man or devil who does not know how to behave himself.'

---

* *cutlass*: a long curved steel blade with a handle, used for cutting vegetation in the Caribbean

It was dark when they slowly walked out of town and took a path which led to the forest. As they approached the forest, they began walking one behind the other, in Indian file, for the track was narrow, and there was the danger of stepping on poisonous snakes hidden under leaves along the way. The old woman led the way, pushing aside a clump of bush in the road now and then to ward off snakes, or occasionally making ringing sounds with her cutlass on the stones in their path. These harsh noises echoed above the tall trees as the early morning gloom lifted. The loud grating noises startled Juanita; she wondered why the old woman made them. Was she deliberately trying to frighten off any evil men or devils who might be peering at two lonely women walking in the deep forest? Juanita did not ask her. She did not want to disturb the chattering of the birds on the tall mahogany trees, or the screeching of monkeys quarrelling and jumping from tree-top to tree-top. Besides, these natural noises were so loud that conversation became almost impossible.

The old woman began to stop occasionally for deep breaths. But Juanita, who was also becoming tired, was impressed by the old woman's strength. They stopped for a rest on a large stone at the side of the track, and had some of the bananas and bread they had brought with them.

'It's going to rain,' said the old woman.

'But the sky is so brilliant!' said Juanita.

'Yes, but it will rain soon; my big toe is restless.'

'Should we not hurry, if all the streams are going to be flooded?' asked Juanita.

'Don't hurry me, you know! I'm an old woman.'

'I'm sorry.' Juanita had forgotten about the old

woman's age because she had walked with such
strength.

'Besides, we're almost there.'

'How do you know?'

'Why do you think we've been slipping and
sliding on those small pebbles along the track?'

'Why?'

'There's a stream nearby.'

'The one with the elf-brook?'

'I think so. Let's get going again.'

After walking in silence for about ten minutes,
they came to a bend in the track. Turning the bend,
they saw a stream with a large basin. A waterfall
was pouring out of the basin, which seemed to
come from a cave in the hillside.

'Here is your elf-brook,' said the old woman.

Excited, with hearts thudding, they approached
the deep pool. Juanita picked out a stone at the
mouth of the pool which lay between two larger
stones, just where the water poured below. She
knew the elf-stone could be the shape of a man, or
a woman, or an animal; this one was definitely the
shape of a man, she thought. She approached it
slowly and picked it up carefully, feeling as though
it might explode in her hand at any time.

'This is the one,' the old woman said, admiring
the stone; 'this is the ugly face of a woman, truly.'
She looked up at the sky.

'No, it is the shape of a man,' said Juanita. She
put the stone in her bag and they began to walk
away from the pool in a hurry. Then something
terrifying happened.

Two stones flew into the air. The first stone hit
Juanita on the back of the head, knocking her
senseless. The second stone hit the old woman
behind her ear and she fell, groggy. As the old

woman lay on the ground, she heard faint voices trying to come through the sound of the rushing stream. Staggering to her feet, she picked up Juanita who was still unconscious and carried her in her arms. She moved quickly, half running, half walking. Juanita still clutched tightly on to her bag.

As the old woman went along, panting heavily, Juanita began to awake with moans of pain. Apart from a small bump where she had been hit, the old woman still felt strong.

When Juanita became fully awake, she looked into the old woman's face and was surprised.

'You're carrying me?' she asked.

'Yes, you were out cold.'

'What happened?'

'The elves threw stones at us. I was hit as well, but not as bad as you.' The old woman stopped for a while to rest.

'How do you feel now?' she asked Juanita.

'My head aches.' Juanita held her head in her hands.

The old woman rubbed Juanita's temples soothingly and said, 'How do you feel now?'

'Better, yes, a lot better.'

'You will be able to walk now,' said the old woman with a deep sigh. 'We have to get to a lonely crossroads. It looks as if it might rain even though the sun is shining.'

They found a lonely crossroads some time later; it was drizzling, but the sun was still shining radiantly. At the lonely crossroads Juanita called forth Roderigo's love. The old woman put Roderigo's picture under the elf-stone and lay it on the ground at the crossroads as it drizzled and the sun shone at the same time. She pointed it in the direction Roderigo usually came riding from. She did not speak until the rain had stopped. Then she buried the picture three feet underground and took the stone away with her. She obtained the promise from Juanita that she would be paid the ten thousand pesos as soon as Juanita and Roderigo were married. She agreed to wait three months for her payment.

The next day, Roderigo, on his tall black horse, came galloping to Juanita's house to ask her to marry him.

After her marriage, Juanita collected money set aside to buy her dresses, in a special account, to pay the old woman. Unfortunately, the bank manager, who was a very good friend of Roderigo, mentioned to him one day that his wife seemed to be creating a large separate account . . . Roderigo questioned Juanita about the money and she told him the truth.

'You must promise never to give anything to that old witch. Do you hear me, Juanita?' Roderigo did not believe in fairies; he knew old folks' sayings and beliefs from his childhood, but he did not believe in such things. He regarded all such matters as nonsense.

'Yes. I understand,' Juanita stuttered.

Roderigo went to see the old woman himself. He was going to end this madness! His wife owed the old woman nothing: she had done nothing for Juanita except take her to the forest and get her stoned!

'Old woman,' he said, when he entered her hut, 'you must promise to leave my wife in peace. I'm not going to pay you a peso!'

'Oh ho! And what about my ten thousand pesos?'

'I don't care about your ten thousand pesos!

It doesn't mean a thing to me! And Juanita is certainly not going to have any dealings with you.'

'So, you want to rob a poor old woman after a fair bargain? You will get what you deserve!'

Roderigo walked away from the old woman's home, confident that he had put an end to her wild claims.

But something happened which put events beyond his control. When he returned to their home, he could not find Juanita anywhere. Two days went by and Juanita could still not be found.

He was frightened and worried, but he knew what he must do. He went back to the old woman's hut. He was the most powerful man in the area and if she knew anything of Juanita's disappearance the old woman would have to reveal it! The old woman showed no surprise when he told her what had happened.

'I warned you to pay your debts!' she said.

They searched the area leading to the elf-pool, Roderigo on horseback, and the old woman on foot. Then the old woman suggested they went to the pool. They moved slowly in the hot afternoon sun! Only the breath of Roderigo's horse broke the stillness of the hour. As soon as they reached the elf-pool and Roderigo descended, the horse became nervous, so Roderigo let it graze in a nearby clearing.

Roderigo went rigid and still as they slowly approached the pool. He could not believe what he saw. There, in the middle of the pool, was Juanita up to her waist in water. Then a small creature with a crown on its head broke the surface beside her and held her hand. It was like a dwarf, with a shrunken, grave face and a long beard. Roderigo rushed into the water to take hold of his wife.

'Juanita, is this you?' he asked, rushing to the place where he had seen her. But he found no one there; he floated to the surface and began to cough. He splashed around looking for Juanita; but she had vanished. After searching for fifteen minutes he came out of the pool shivering with cold and very afraid.

'It was my Juanita!' he said as he stood next to the old woman looking at the centre of the pool again.

'Are you sure?' asked the old woman mockingly.

'Of course I'm sure, I saw her . . . and . . . that creature.'

'Oh, what creature?'

'That little pint-sized monster! It was my Juanita I tell you! Please, I want her back.'

'And how much is it worth to you?'

'All right, you old witch! I will pay you your ten thousand pesos.'

'I want twenty thousand!'

'Here you are . . . you wife of the devil!' Roderigo took out a cheque book and wrote out a cheque for twenty thousand pesos.

'If the bank does not pay me tomorrow I will not be responsible for what happens,' she said.

'You will get your money! Now give me my wife!'

'I don't have your wife. Look, there she is.' And there was Juanita rising out of the water escorted by the elf-king again. The elf-king brought her to the edge of the pool, saluted Roderigo, then returned to the centre of the pool where he disappeared.

Roderigo found no trace of water on Juanita as he embraced her.

'And you still don't believe in fairies?' the old

woman asked Roderigo. Roderigo did not answer. Instead, he helped Juanita on to his horse and he climbed on behind her. The old woman walked ahead of them, her face glowing triumphantly in the early-morning sun.

THE LITTLE GIRL SAVED BY HER FATHER

(from Haiti)

ALEX-LOUISE TESSONNEAU

Translated by Bridget Jones

ONCE THERE was a man from *Le Cap** who was
unemployed. He wrote off to *Port-au-Prince*†
to ask for a job, and as soon as the answer came,
he called his wife to him and said:

'My dear, the time has come for me to go away.
I'm going to make some money for myself and all
the children, so I'm going away to work. The first
month-end I'll send you money, so that you and
all the children can come and join me in Port-au-
Prince. Bring all your children and that little
daughter of mine who is your stepchild.'

And he added:

'I've seen how nicely you get on with my daughter when I am here. When I'm away, I want you to
treat her ten times better.'

Now the woman began to weep and wail (but
you know really she was just pretending) and
said:

'See here now, you've no right at all to tell
me this, that is quite out of order. You've seen

---

* *Le Cap*: a town in the north of Haiti
† *Port-au-Prince*: the capital city of Haiti

how well I care for your daughter when you are watching, behind your back I'll do better still.' (She used to say a whole lot of things like that.)

'All right, all right, darling, you don't need to carry on so. I'm only saying that; I've seen how you live with my little one, of course I have.'

The man set out and went off to Port-au-Prince for that job of his.

And do you know what that woman did? She was the stepmother, remember, and the very same day that her husband took the bus to Port-au-Prince, she hurried and took the bus herself. She went to the house of a *galipot*,* so that at the stroke of midnight, Galipot would come and take away the little girl. Yes, to carry off the man's little daughter at midnight, that's what Galipot arranged, saying:

'What you're going to do is this. You have two children, don't you? When you see the lamps light up, about six o'clock, send them out to play *lago*† under the light-pole. When they're going to play, you'll arrange with your own children to cheat at drawing straws for turns, so that the man's daughter has to be the catcher. She'll cover her eyes and they'll hide. But when they're hiding, they'll come home into your house, and you'll stop up the windows and door. The man's daughter must stay outside, because I can't go indoors to take her. I can capture her outside, everything out there in the night belongs to me.'

Not a soul in the world knew about it, but that little girl was born with a star on her forehead. Her mother didn't know, her father didn't know, only

---

* *galipot*: in Haiti a supernatural being that sucks blood
† *lago*: a game resembling hide-and-seek

God knew about that star on her head. The star was her protection. As she grew, so did its power, but it was a secret from everyone.

And in no time at all, guess what, six o'clock came around, and the little girl was asked to play Iago. She, all innocent, the others scheming together, so that when they picked turns holding a little stone and it came out that she was to hide, the others said:

'No, that's wrong.'

They cheated (to make quite sure that she had to seek them) and said to her:

'Close your eyes!'

Then they went off to hide, but what they really did was run off home into their mother's house, and she wedged the door tight shut.

The little girl stayed outside. She didn't suspect that the other two were indoors: if you're playing a game, you've no right to run off home and leave the others. So she began the game, hunting for them high and low, up and down, all over the neighbourhood, never catching one glimpse of those children. For all her seeking she couldn't see the others, and all alone she called out: 'Red rooster! Red rooster!' as if there were several children with her. But it wasn't true, there weren't any others playing with her, she was just hoping to reach her stepmother's children where they were hidden and bring them out. But that could never be, they were already fast asleep snuggled up against their mother's belly.

So the little girl was left outside alone.

Even the neighbours coming in from the street, closing their street doors, realized that she was going to have to sleep outside, but they didn't want to take her into their homes. Suppose tomorrow morning the stepmother claimed that the girl had run off with some money? Then those who had given her a roof for the night would have to pay back the money. They resigned themselves to being hard-hearted. The little girl was going to sleep in the street. Right away they knew that meant misfortune. Then eleven o'clock began to strike. The little girl looked up and down the street: not a living soul to be seen. She was all alone outside. She couldn't believe the others had left her, and went on looking, till pop! she saw it was twenty to twelve.

She looked up and down. Nobody there! She went to the passage door and saw that she could pull it open towards her. All the other doors were tight shut. She went into the yard and shut the passage door behind her. (But there was something like a great big stone lurking just opposite stepmother's room door...) She pulled at stepmother's door, but she found it was shut tight, and she was just standing outside when, Dong! Dong! Midnight struck! There was a cock on top of a tree and he sang:

'Cockadoodledoo!'

Galipot jumped at the little girl – Pow! – to snatch her up.

The star blazed out of the little girl's head – Pow! – and struck Galipot such a blow – Pow! Pow! – that it was knocked clean out of here and on to the top of the mountains at Le Cap. It was then that the little girl looked and saw what danger she was in, and she began to sing and beat upon stepmother's door, knock, knock, knock! She sang:

'Stepmother, stepmother
Open the door

Before the cock a crow
Hear me here and hear me there
Stepmother, the devil's going to gobble me
    up.'

And stepmother answered, saying:

'Let the devil eat you up
Let him eat
If you see the devil
Coming to gobble you up
Fight the devil yourself!'

And she added: 'Go call your daddy, then, you're his blood!'

The little girl sank down. Galipot got ready to attack her again, coming run, run, run, to get her this time.

The cock crowed, 'Cockadoodledoo!'

Galipot went for the little girl again – Pow!

The star came out again: Baf! another blow.

The star knocked Galipot away over into Vertière District. But each blow at Galipot weakened the star. Just seven blows and all its strength would be gone and the little girl as good as dead.

By the fifth blow the star was growing weaker still, and could send Galipot no further than from here to Guinea District.

Galipot was getting set for the final charge, yes, sir!

Meanwhile, the girl's father was working away in Port-au-Prince in a diesel oil depot, and around those tanks no fly or wasp or bee was ever to be seen. Papa saw a bee coming for him, and that bee stung him – Zip! Papa said:

'Now what do you think this bee is doing here?

Here I am working with the diesel fuel; how can this bring out a bee to come and sting me?'

Papa said:

'I must go and consult the wise man to find out what this means.'

Straightaway he asked permission to go for a consultation. *'Braps!'** Papa went off to get his fortune told. He hardly got to where the *bocor*† was, before the wise man said:

'Oh dear, my friend, you're in danger!'

He went on:

'You just have one little daughter, and that very same day you left and took the bus for Port-au-Prince, her stepmother had plotted with a galipot to come and suck her blood dry! Yes!'

And he said:

'By good fortune your daughter was born with a star on her forehead, and that's why Galipot hasn't been able to take her yet. But there are only two strikes left, the star has only two blows left to protect her, the star is weakening fast and when . . .'

The man cried out:

'What?'

The bocor said to him:

'Can you handle a gun?'

The fellow said:

'Yes, I'm very good at shooting.'

'Good. I'm going to send you back to Le Cap. I'm going to give you a gun and just one cartridge. (I'm sending you to kill that Galipot.) If you are unlucky, if you don't shoot and kill, Galipot will get your little daughter and you as well.'

---

* *Braps!*: exclamation of suddenness
† *bocor*: the priest of the Vodoun cult, especially in his role as a clairvoyant and diviner

Without hesitation the man said yes, he could shoot straight. He said: 'OK, let's go.'

In those far-off days, there wasn't a plane. The man didn't have any time to spare, the bocor knew the star only had two blows left. He said:

'Right, I am sending you off.'

Then he gave the man a riding whip and said:

'Go to my stable. Crack the whip three times on the stable door, then take the whip and throw it across inside. The animal that it lands on you must take out and use for your journey.'

The man trusted the bocor, so he slung the gun on his back, took the whip and came to the stable door:

Crack! Crack! Crack!

And then he tossed up the whip, and what did it fall upon but a little skinny donkey. A donkey so thin that he could pass between two drops of rain without getting wet.

The man said:

'Oh dear!'

The man said:

'Do you think this little donkey can travel that long, long road?'

But he trusted the bocor, so he went in and took the little donkey and saddled him up – and well, you've heard how a plane goes? I tell you that donkey went faster than any jet.

When the man reached Le Cap on his little donkey, he didn't dash straight into the house. He didn't run inside, he waited outside in ambush.

The star had only two strikes left before it would fade right out. The little girl beat upon the door:

Knock, knock, knock, knock! Knock, knock, knock!

She sang:

'Stepmother, stepmother
Open the door
Before the cock a crow
Hear me here and hear me there
Stepmother, the devil's going to gobble me
    up.'

Stepmother answered:

'Let the devil eat you up
Let him eat
If you see the devil
Coming to gobble you up
Fight the devil yourself!'

The cock crowed: 'Cockadoodledoo!'
Galipot sprang at the little girl – Pow!
The star went: Baf!
The star was losing its strength, it could only
just knock Galipot out of the yard, its heart was
failing, it had no power left.
    The little girl began to cry, her eyes filled with
tears, she begged:

'Stepmother, stepmother
Open the door
Before the cock a crow
Hear me here and hear me there
Stepmother, the devil's going to gobble me
    up.'

Stepmother answered:

'Let the devil eat you up
Let him eat
If you see the devil

Coming to gobble you up
Fight the devil yourself!'

The cock crowed: 'Cockadoodledoo!'
Galipot lunged – Pow! at the little girl.
Bang! went the gun.
Papa killed the galipot.
Papa came running.
He had a *couline** at his waist. He pulled it out, and – Chak! – he forced out the door. He opened the barrier, took up his daughter and came out. He caught hold of the galipot, dragged away the body and threw it under a bridge. Then he went off with his daughter.

At that moment he was so full of indignation, he went off to find a shop. He knocked and they let him in and he bought two bottles of petrol and two boxes of matches, and he looked for a ladder.

Now stepmother didn't know what was going on outside, she was sleeping deeply with her two little ones.

Father set up the ladder, and climbed on to her house, there where the stepmother slept with her two little ones, and he took his daughter with him. He gave her one bottle of petrol and he kept one, she had one box of matches and he had one. He said to her:

'Here's what you must do: sprinkle the petrol around below and start the fire. I'm going to sprinkle the petrol up here and set it alight. When the two meet, we come down.'

And so they did: daughter down below and Papa on top, spreading the petrol and starting the fire. And when they met, he took her and came down,

---

* *couline*: a kind of machete

and set out again with her for Port-au-Prince.
   Then the house burnt down with stepmother
and her two children inside.

   And that's where they gave me one little kick
   Right out of the basket and into the bottle.

THE DEVIL'S AGENT

(from French Guiana)

JEAN POPEAU

THE OWNER of a sawmill was returning to La Compte from Cayenne, the capital of French Guiana, when he came upon a green coral snake in his path. It was near twilight; the sun was rapidly descending behind the trees and he was in a hurry to get home.

The snake lifted its head and asked: 'Why are you in such a hurry, stranger?' The man was afraid but he tried not to show it. He had been told stories by his grandmother of the strange creatures which dwell in the jungles of French Guiana. 'Some of them bar your path and speak to you,' she had insisted.

'I'm going home to save my business,' the man replied quite naturally.

'I can see you're worried,' said the snake.

'So would you be if you had just borrowed ten thousand dollars from the bank.'

'To save your business?'

'It's my last gamble; after that I'll probably cut my throat!'

'I don't think you'll need to cut your throat. This is what you have to do . . .'

The snake gave the man detailed advice on how

to invest the money to save his business. The man was grateful but anxious: he knew he would have to repay the snake in some way.

'What is it you want in return?' he asked.

'You have a son: he's stupid, he drinks all the time, he's a time-waster, he's evil . . .'

'You can have that blasted vagabond!' the man shouted.

The snake slithered into the jungle. The man was not to know that the 'snake' was *Maskalili*.* The man used the money just as Maskalili had advised, and the business prospered. He soon became rich. In the enjoyment of his riches, he forgot the pact with Maskalili. He sent his son to France for an expensive education.

Maskalili went to the business man's house and slithered to the stream where the household collected their water. At this point, I should tell you that Maskalili meant to play a trick on the man. Maskalili always plays tricks on people who enter into bargains with him. It is his way of proving he is not to be trusted. Those who trust in him are always deceived. He changes all the time. If you accuse him of cheating, he can always say, 'It was not *me* you made the bargain with, it was my other self of yesterday!' Maskalili was going to steal the man's beautiful daughter, instead of the silly son whom the sawmill owner expected him to take. Just to prove what a devil he was!

Totally unaware of Maskalili's intentions, the man sent his daughter to the stream every day in the afternoon sunshine to fetch water. She was a beautiful Indian girl. He saw her and immediately, Maskalili's heart was smitten. When she came to

* *Maskalili*: servant of the devil

fetch water for what he knew would be the last time that day, he changed into his human, four-year-old child form. He was dressed in a black suit with trousers that trailed the ground. The sun began to fall behind the trees beside their house, and she heard his cry: 'pip-pip-lili!' He walked slowly to her. She was startled but not alarmed. She placed her bucket down and took his small hand, and together they walked into the darkness.

The man searched the entire neighbourhood for his daughter. Then he went to the local police chief who was his friend. 'I'm sorry, my friend,' said the police chief, 'but I cannot even begin a search for the child. I have only one man to help me with this miserable police station, and I'm getting more and more cases like yours coming in.' The police chief told the man of an army barracks fifty miles away from which he could hire some soldiers as a search party.

Stricken with grief, the man took all the money he had and even put up half the business for sale. Only one person came forward to buy this half-share in the man's business. He was a handsome dwarf-like stranger, dressed in black, who came riding on horseback. Yes, it was Maskalili. The stranger explained he had heard that the man had lost his daughter and was eager to help him. He offered to lead the search party, saying that he knew the surrounding area very well. The man was impressed by the stranger's sincerity and kindness.

Together with the stranger, the man went to the army barracks to hire fifty soldiers for two months. When he heard the man's story, and looked at the stranger, the army commander would not take him seriously at first.

'Tell me the truth, Mr Man,' he said, 'you're making a movie and you want fifty extras! And what part is he playing?' he asked, pointing at the stranger.

'He is going to lead the search party. Captain, I assure you, I'm going to look for my daughter!'

'He going dressed like this?' asked the captain, laughing, pointing at Maskalili: 'He going to play the devil himself!'

'Please, captain!' shouted the man, sobbing.

'OK, OK. They say a fool and his money are soon parted. You have plenty money and you're a fool. Lieutenant!'

A smart young lieutenant came marching into the room.

'Lieutenant,' said the commander: 'I want you to take fifty men and go with this man to look for . . . to look for . . . the chief devil-in-the-woods! No, no, no, to look for his daughter! That's it, to look for his daughter. He will pay all expenses. You understand?'

'Yes sir!' shouted the lieutenant.

'This little devil here will be your guide,' said the commander, without thinking, pointing at the stranger.

'Who, sir?' asked the lieutenant.

'I mean this little half-man here. This little fellow here.'

'Captain, this man is my friend. Please treat him with respect,' said the business man.

'Yes, yes, excuse me, sir,' said the captain, 'I had a hard night last night, I don't know what the devil got into me! Ha, ha!'

The search party left the army base led by the stranger in black, riding at the front in the burning sunshine. The business man rode at the back of the party. They rode into the forest and looked like dwarfs among the giant multi-coloured trees. They got off their horses and struggled with them up difficult hills, with trees digging their twisted roots into soft earth. The young man seemed to know which path to take and which to avoid. *He* seemed to be the leader of the group, not the lieutenant in command. The business man followed Maskalili's movements carefully. He was becoming very impressed by the young man's instinctive knowledge of the area and his sureness of foot.

As for the lieutenant, he was obviously firmly in control of his men, and they obeyed him completely. The men were all experienced soldiers. They made good progress, cutting away at the dense undergrowth when it got in their way. But there was something about the young stranger which made the lieutenant uneasy. Perhaps it was the fact that he spoke so seldom. And then there were the tracks he left as he walked. No one could see what he wore on his feet because his trousers were so long. But the lieutenant had never seen such footmarks before. They were quite faint and the others did not seem to have noticed them. The lieutenant had become interested because as an ex-scout, he naturally looked at the ground for animal tracks. He had at first mistaken the young man's tracks for those of a strange animal. But now he was in no doubt. As soon as convenient, he must take a look at the young stranger's feet!

They travelled deeper into the forest. Sometimes they heard strange cries and they thought that they must be the noise of howler monkeys, or mournful parrots. Sometimes the cry sounded like the pitiful protest of a prey, wailing for its few last moments.

They all heard a loud cry cut the air one night, just as they were eating round a camp-fire. The man thought it was the cry of his daughter; it seemed to say: 'Papa, Papa!' The man's heart was full of sorrow, yet hopeful.

The lieutenant came to sit beside the man and watched his troubled face in the dim light.

'I think I heard my daughter,' the man said.

'So many days and no sign of her,' said the lieutenant; 'maybe it is your guide.'

'He's a kind young fellow and I trust him,' said the man.

'Yes, but what kind of a fellow is he?' asked the lieutenant.

'What do you mean?' the man asked.

'Have you seen his tracks?' the lieutenant asked.

'I'm not interested in his foot,' said the man.

'Only one creature has footmarks like that,' whispered the lieutenant.

'What?'

'Maskalili,' the lieutenant whispered. 'He will prowl round your hut at night whistling, "pip-pip-lili". If you call out his name, he'll stop whistling. He feeds on green coffee beans and pimentos. If you have a bush of fruit when you go to bed, you might find them gone in the morning. Maskalili has paid you a visit! He has the strangest tracks you ever saw.'

'Wait! Stop!' the man whispered.

'Do you want to tell me something?' asked the lieutenant.

'No! I have nothing to tell you.'

'Well, I swear to God, before the night is out,

I'm going to find this young boy's secret!' The lieutenant seemed determined.

The man was afraid to tell the lieutenant about his meeting with the snake, months previously. He was afraid that any sharing of his secret would mean the final loss of his daughter. He had the feeling if he revealed anything of his meeting with the creature, something dreadful would happen to her. Something dreadful may already have happened, but he felt if he spoke up, it would happen for certain. He did not want to risk the destruction of his own daughter. But could that young man be the 'Maskalili' that the lieutenant was talking about? Surely not! He seemed much too kind and genuine to be a fiend in disguise. Yet the young man spoke so little. Even the captain had spoken of him as a devil! Still, those were only words: words like that were in common everyday use. The man went to sleep with his head full of words.

That night, the man dreamt about his daughter; she appeared to him dressed all in white, as beautiful as on the day she had disappeared. She spoke in a strange, yet happy voice: 'Don't worry Papa, I'll be seeing you soon.' He spoke her name, then he woke up. The dream troubled him and he felt he must tell someone about his secret meeting with the snake. It was becoming too much to bear. The lieutenant! Yes, he would tell the lieutenant after all!

But the next day he was horrified by what he found. As he gazed up at the individual shafts of early morning light, like dozens of spotlights from the sky, each dim ray of light seemed to pick out a soldier lying dead on the ground. He walked to the lieutenant; he was dead also. They were all dead. The young man and his horse were gone. Terrified and full of grief, the man began walking crazily back to his home.

Many days later, he reached his home. His son came to the door to greet him. He had forgotten all about his son. The boy was shocked at his father's appearance; he looked very old and dirty and had a long beard.

'My sister has been here,' the son said.

'Your what?'

'My sister. She came with her boyfriend, a good-looking, short young man. I cooked a meal for them, then they went on their way.'

'How dare you make fun of your sister's disappearance!' shouted the man.

'But Papa, I'm telling you she was here!'

'Stop telling lies, you depraved monster! You were always good for nothing! Pack your bags and get out!' The man sent the boy on his way.

He began to live in the house alone. Every afternoon, he had a vision of his daughter walking down the nearby mountain in a long flowing white dress, carrying a basket of food in her hand. She seemed very happy. He was forever hopeful that she would return to the house.

One day, he visited the spot where he had seen her in his visions. He found tracks just like those of Maskalili. He went home for his gun and went back to the tracks. He was going to shoot Maskalili. Maskalili had taken away his only daughter! He followed the tracks all day until they led him to a clump of trees in a clearing in the woods. As he entered among the trees he saw a figure dart out. Just like Maskalili! He shot at the figure on impulse. It fell. He ran to where the figure lay on the other side of the trees in the clearing. What he saw at first startled, then sickened him. He picked up the figure and began to howl with grief. It was his own daughter.

THE WOMAN IN BLACK

(from Guadeloupe)

JEAN POPEAU

Two young men from the capital of Guadeloupe, Bass-Terre, were on holiday in a small
village in the countryside. One of them was looking out over the village square when he called to
the other.

'Heh! Jean-Pierre, come and look at a beautiful
Guadeloupean woman.'

'You're right,' said Paul, Jean-Pierre's friend. 'I've
never seen such a beautiful woman in these parts
before.'

Jean-Pierre whistled to her and shouted: 'Heh!
beauty! where are you going, and can I go with
you?'

She did not answer, but went into a house on
the edge of the square.

Both of the young men had just arrived at the
village, and Paul was the one who was particularly
tired from the journey. He decided to take an
afternoon nap, while Jean-Pierre sat on the veranda
with a strong whiskey. The drink and the heat
were already beginning to affect his senses when he
saw the young woman walking out of the village.

She had reached the outskirts of the village when
he caught up with her. She was carrying a basket

of goods on her head. The midday sun was blazing down unremittingly and the glaring light made everything around assume a peculiar white pallor.

Paul, meanwhile, was having a strange dream. That same young woman was the main figure in his dream. He could see her clearly. There was something strange about her which made the dreamer uneasy.

'Jean-Pierre!' In his dream, he called out in alarm.

Jean-Pierre was walking in the blazing sun beside the young woman, who balanced her basket as gracefully as a seal keeping a ball on its nose.

'Where are you going, my dear?' asked Jean-Pierre.

'Affairs of the centipede are not affairs of the goat,' she replied.

'But why are you dressed so, all in black?' he asked.

'I'm mourning my dead soul,' she answered.

'Eh, eh! Is that so? Where are you going now?' They walked out of the village.

'My love is gone. I go after my love,' she replied.

'Ah, so you have a lover, eh?' he asked.

'The crab gives a dance. The lizard comes un-invited!' she answered.

'Come, come, my dear. Tell me where you're going, sweetheart!' Jean-Pierre pleaded in mock despair.

'As far as the land of the lizard!' she smiled sweetly.

'That is many miles,' Jean-Pierre answered in the same mocking spirit as though he knew where she meant.

'Does it matter? Are you coming with me?' This was an invitation Jean-Pierre secretly could not resist. She was so beautiful! He would have walked to the other end of Guadeloupe with her. He had nothing else to do.

'What is your name, *doudou*?'* Jean-Pierre asked.

'Guess!' she challenged him.

'Is it Christophine?'

'No, it's not that!'

'Is it Juliana?'

'No, it's not that – silly!'

'Is it Ziza?'

'No! Try again!'

'Is it Julietta?'

'No, no!'

'Ah, it's Nini!'

'No, you're the ninny! Try again, pretty boy.'

'Is it Florestin?'

'No. Tell me, what do you want my name for? What are you going to do with it?'

'I want to know your secret, darling. I think your secret is in your name.'

She began to sing a strange yet happy song with one main refrain, 'I have been sleeping too long'. Jean-Pierre could not make much of it. He was too busy trying to keep up with her. His thin clothing was already drenched with sweat, while she walked on, coolly and gracefully, with no sign of sweat on her beautiful skin. She laughed mockingly at his desperate efforts to keep up with her in the blazing heat, saying: 'Just stay behind me, my dear, always behind!' And as if bewitched by the supple movements of her body, he followed her like a prey charmed by a cobra.

The sun began to fall behind the mountains as he still continued to follow her, chatting and

* *doudou*: a term of endearment, like 'darling'

laughing and singing bits of songs with her along
the way. When they came to villages, she walked
through them without speaking to anyone, and he
did the same. They left the valley and began to
climb the mountains, and as the day wore on, their
shadows lengthened. Their shadows extended
from their feet, sometimes mixing, sometimes
climbing up trees, and sometimes fading into the
growing darkness. The woman then left the main
path.

She left the path so suddenly, that he had hardly
noticed that they were on the top of the mountain.
He hesitated for a moment and saw the sun disappear. They were completely enveloped in darkness,
and he wondered where she was going. 'Where are
you going?' he shouted. 'What is the matter with
you!' she answered. 'The road is shorter this way.'
'It may be shorter, but the snakes, the *fer-de-
lance*!'* he cried. 'No snakes along this way,' she
said. 'I should know, I've used this path often
enough!'

For some time he could make out her figure
ahead of him with her white head-kerchief. He now
remembered she had been wearing a head-kerchief
when he first met her. After a while, the path
zigzagged into shadows and he could not see her
any more. 'Where are you?' he shouted. 'I can't see
anything.' 'Here,' she said, 'hold my hand.' Why
did her hand feel so cold, he wondered – just like
that of a strange animal! She walked swiftly, as
though she knew the path by heart.

That afternoon, at about the time that his friend
had left with the young woman, Paul woke with
a strange fright. He knew Jean-Pierre had left the

---

* *fer-de-lance*: a type of poisonous snake

village. He had seen it in his dream! But that was all he could remember – that they had left together. He couldn't remember anything else but that. He knew only that he had this strange feeling in his guts: whatever had happened to Jean-Pierre was too horrifying even to think about.

He took the road leading out of the village, the same road that his friend and the young woman had taken. The road led him to a small village where he met an old man. He questioned the old man, asking him if he had seen Jean-Pierre and a beautiful woman walking towards his village. He explained how he had gone to take a nap and had left his friend gazing at the village square. He was sure his friend had gone down to speak to the beautiful young woman.

'Why of course, you may be right,' said the old man. 'Sometimes they look like people, like beautiful people.'

'Who look like people?' asked Paul.

'*Zombies** of course,' said the old man, in a matter-of-fact tone of voice. 'I can see you're not from around here.'

Paul confirmed that he and Jean-Pierre were on holiday from the capital.

'Have you ever seen one?' asked Paul, returning to the zombies.

'Have I ever seen one! I see them almost every day. Sometimes they walk about my room at night. They walk like people. They sit in my rocking chair and rock very softly, and look at me. I say to them: "What do you want from me? I never did you any harm. Go away!" Then they go away.'

'You know who they are?' Paul asked.

* *zombies*: corpses revived by witchcraft

'Of course I know who they are! They're my
neighbours, they're from this village, and from the
other villages. They can disguise themselves as
they like, I know them! Sometimes they're fireflies.'

'You mean those things we call "La Belle"?'

'If I see one of those in my room, I catch it and
put it in the piss pot!' said the old man. 'This
morning I saw a crab. A crab walking in the middle
of the village, just before daybreak! I said to it:
"You'd better find yourself home before dawn
catches you!"'

The old man began to ponder.

'Searching through my mind, I remember a
young man and a woman dressed in black. They
passed this way not an hour ago. They took the
road to the next village. If I see them again, I will
report it to you.'

Paul told the old man how to find the house
where he was staying. The old man seemed to
know it. There was nothing he didn't know about
the villages around the place, he said. He pointed
Paul to the next village two miles away, and told
him to enquire about his friend there.

'Say Mr Lugaroo sent you,' said the old man,
'they know me well!'

After speaking to the old man, Paul was even more
afraid for the fate of his friend than he had at first been.
He reached the next village just after midday. He saw
that it was called Mourne Rouge, which means Red
Mountain. The first person he met was a young boy.
He was killing a centipede.

'Let me kill you, Satan!' shouted the boy, beating
the creature's head with a stone. The boy was
beside himself with anger. Paul asked him why he
was killing the centipede.

'It's a zombie, and it's evil!' said the boy. 'If you kill a centipede you might win plenty of money. Even if you dream of killing one it's good luck!'

Paul asked him whether he had seen a young man and a beautiful woman coming into the village.

'I saw a man and a woman, just as you say, around half an hour ago,' said the boy. 'The woman was dressed in black! I sorry for your friend!'

The boy pointed Paul to the route the couple had taken, which led to the next village.

As he approached that village, Paul met an old woman carrying a basket of ground provisions. He offered to help her with the load but she declined his help: she said she was probably more used to carrying loads than he was – she could tell by his appearance. She was wearing a long purple dress which trailed on the ground. Had a young man and a beautiful woman passed her on her journey, Paul asked her.

'Yes, you'll have to hurry if you want to catch them,' she said. 'It will be dark soon.'

Paul explained that his friend had followed the woman out of the village. He was in despair; they did not seem to have stopped anywhere.

'Maybe she is a zombie,' the old woman said, mockingly.

Paul gave her a long searching look, up and down.

'Don't look at me, you know! I'm not a zombie! If you meet a horse at night, with only three legs, that is a zombie! If you see a fire filling the road at night, and as you approach, it moves away from you, that is zombie! If you follow that fire, it will lead you into a chasm, a precipice.'

Paul did not speak for some time; the old

woman's mocking, playful tone put great fear into him.

'How can such a beautiful woman be a zombie?' he asked.

'Ah, sir, a zombie can change into anything! Into a dog, or a horse, or an old woman, or a donkey. So why not into a beautiful woman? If you find a donkey in the middle of the road at night, this is what you do. You climb on it backwards, grab its tail, and tell it to take you home!'

'How can you climb on a donkey backwards?' asked Paul.

'You foolish or what!' said the old woman. 'Approach the donkey backwards. Keep your back to it all the time. Tell it to squat down. Say, "I know who you are, and what you are!"'

'But supposing you don't know who it is?'

'It doesn't know that! Once you speak those words it will do what you tell it.'

'Your friend did not stop here,' the old woman told Paul when they reached the village.

'Walk fast, you'll catch them!'

Paul wondered how she knew they had not stopped. He was becoming frantic about Jean-Pierre's fate. He tried to guess what had happened to his friend. He couldn't.

The young woman had still not revealed her name to Jean-Pierre, but by now he was in love with her. He was completely enchanted. They were at the top of a mountain and he could see a small stream below in the moonlight. She still held his hands, and the woman's face was even more beautiful in moonlight than in daylight.

'Darling, who are you?' he asked.

She laughed mockingly.

'Do you love me?' she asked playfully.

'Oh yes, yes, I'll follow you always,' he said.

'Do you?' she again asked.

'Yes, you know I do, you know, my love.'

She led him to the edge of the mountain, and the moonlight lit up the brightness of her beauty.

'Kiss me,' she said.

He bent forward to kiss her. She gave out a harsh shriek of laughter and pushed him over the edge.

Paul had still been searching in the darkness when he heard the deathly cry of the man falling over the edge of the precipice. He went back to the village and organized a search party. The villagers soon led him to the body of his friend lying in the stream. As they saw to the broken body, Paul looked up to the edge of the precipice. He saw a face lit in a crimson light. The face then disappeared with a shriek of laughter.

PIERRE AND THE LA DIABLESSE

(from Martinique)

FAUSTIN CHARLES

PIERRE AND his mother Ma Gautier lived in a wooden house with a veranda at the front in a country village. Pierre was a watchman. Sometimes during the day, Pierre used to fish in the sea: he was very good at it. But Pierre had a problem, or so he thought. He was very ugly and he was ashamed of it. Had it not been for his mother who pleaded with him not to stop fishing, he would have given it up. He had no friends and hardly went out in the daytime. Pierre was thirty years old, the youngest and only survivor of five sons; his four brothers and father had died when he was a teenager.

Pierre was always depressed and his mother consoled and tried to cheer him up. One day they were having lunch when Pierre said angrily,

'I not going fishing any more.'

'Boy, why you worry so much?' said his mother. 'You born that way, there's nothing you can do to change that. I glad at least I have one son living. I does thank the Lord for that.'

'But mama, I is a big man, and I don't have a girlfriend.' Pierre stared misty-eyed at the food on his plate. 'I mean, which woman will want to marry me? They don't even want to look at me, so how I will ever have a woman friend?'

'Don't worry, I tell you,' his mother comforted. 'One day you will meet a woman who wouldn't care how you look, she going to like you for what you is inside. Remember, is the mind of a person that does make the person.'

'But mama, they does make jokes at me,' Pierre said roughly. 'They does say that is the devil make me, that I is ugly as sin.'

'Never mind them, my son, is God make you, and he know why he make you so. Pay no attention to them stupid people.'

'I does feel sometime that it's me who shoulda dead instead of me brothers, they wasn't as ugly as me. I don't have nothing to live for.'

'Oh Lord, it does hurt me bad when you talk like that,' said Ma Gautier with tears in her eyes. 'If you did dead, I woulda be all by meself. No, me son, you mustn't say things like that.'

'All right, mama, me sorry,' said Pierre, playing with a spoon, 'but I'll always be a bachelor. I never going to have children. And you never going to have grandchildren.'

'No, boy, I tell you don't say that. Everybody in this world have their partner; it's like the saying: "every bread has its cheese"; so you just have to keep faith, me son.'

'You only trying to make me feel good, mama,' said Pierre, picking at his food.

'What else you want me to do, boy?' his mother's lips trembled. 'You is me one and only son.' Ma Gautier did not feel hungry but she forced herself to eat.

Pierre kept watch on the site where a new primary school was being built; it was partly finished.

He sat on a bench with a torchlight in his hand in one of the completed parts. He was deep in thought when a woman's voice greeted him, 'Hello, man! No don't shine the light on me. I don't like light, bright light does hurt me eyes. I not a thief, I just come to keep you company, that's all. I notice you does be all alone here.'

Pierre was completely taken aback. Who was the woman? Maybe she was making fun of him? Then he thought that she was only speaking to him because she could not see his ugly face in the darkness. He decided against shining the torchlight on her.

'What you want around here?' he asked, a little impatient.

'I tell you me not trespassing. I don't like to see people lonely, it not right.'

'This is me work. I is a watchman. I have to be here by meself,' Pierre's voice was arrogant.

The woman came closer and Pierre smelt the perfume she was wearing. It was very sweet and intoxicating and as it began to have an effect on him, he relaxed, and said, 'What you doing out so late?'

'Well, I was feeling lonely, so me decide to go for a walk,' replied the woman, coming closer. 'I hope I not bothering you, it's nice to have somebody to talk to.'

The woman's manner was so charming, so trusting, that Pierre became captivated by her. He put down the torchlight in front of him, folded his arms, and said, 'No, you not bothering me. It's just I have to be careful in me job.'

'Yes, yes, I know that. It's a very lonely job, though.'

'You live in this village?' Pierre asked sombrely.

'No, I not from around here, but it's so nice in
this village, I does come here for a walk. Sometimes
I does go for walks by the seaside as well.'

'Yes, it's a nice village,' Pierre said, turning away
shyly.

'You wife like you doing this kinda work?' the
woman asked tactfully.

'I not married. I living with me mother.' Pierre
was a bit annoyed.

'I not married either,' the woman sighed. 'I still
waiting for the right man to come along. The
only thing me will want him to know and always
remember is, I don't like light, it not good for me
eyes.'

'I don't care for it much, meself,' said Pierre,
putting a hand over his face. 'Anyway, one of these
days, you going to find a nice husband.'

Even in the darkness, Pierre sensed that the
woman was beautiful. She was wearing a long,
flowing flowery-patterned dress which touched
the floor. Pierre was always told that he had very
good eyesight and that he could see in the dark
extremely well; he was staring hard at the woman,
when she remarked, 'Everybody does tell me that
I is a very pretty lady, and plenty men does chat
me up, but me doesn't pay no attention to them.'

'That's because you is a decent woman,' Pierre
said curtly. 'Me mother tell me to respect people
like yourself.'

'Thank you for you compliment,' the woman
said happily. 'By the way, is how long you doing
this kinda work?'

'For some years,' Pierre answered anxiously.
'The pay is all right. All I have to do is see that
nobody steal the galvanized iron, the timber or the
cement.'

'I feeling in me heart that you is a kind fellar,' the woman said cheerfully. 'I know when I meet a nice man.'

Pierre winced, fidgeted, bowed his head, and muttered, 'Thank you for saying that. That's very nice of you.'

'I mean it, and me sure we going to be very good friends. Well, I have to go now, see you tomorrow night, bye, bye.' And she laughed, turned and went away.

'Bye, bye, see you,' Pierre stuttered. He was overjoyed for at last he had found a woman friend. He could not wait to tell his mother about it. But his joy turned to sorrow when he began to think how the woman would react when she saw his ugly face. He put it out of his mind and decided to enjoy the friendship while it lasted.

The following morning, he told his mother all about the woman, 'Mama, she very nice, and decent. You know, you was right, at last I think I find a woman.'

'She from the village?' his mother asked suspiciously.

'No, she not from around here,' Pierre answered happily.

'She see you face?' his mother's tone was discouraging.

'No, you know it was dark. And she tell me not to shine light on she because she afraid of bright light, it does hurt she eyes.'

'She sounds like a nice person, but me don't know.' His mother seemed unhappy.

'Mama, you not happy for me,' Pierre was surprised. 'You should be happy for me. You always tell me that one day I going to meet a girl, now I meet a girl, you don't like it.'

Ma Gautier did not want to hurt her son's feelings, but at the same time she did not want any harm to come to him.

'I glad for you, me son,' she said, sighing heavily. 'Maybe I worrying for nothing, but is the way you meet the woman; I don't know, it seem kinda strange.'

'Well, you can wish me well,' Pierre forced a smile as he spoke. 'Okay, so we meet in the dark, but that suit me fine, she don't like light, and I don't care for it either. I don't want she to see me face.'

'But boy, how you talking so foolish. The time going to come when she'll have to see you face.'

'I not letting that worry me,' said Pierre who did not care. 'Before the time come when she see me face, I going to enjoy the friendship. I mean, what wrong with a little make-believe, it better than nothing.'

'That's up to you, boy,' said his mother worriedly.

'I was thinking that maybe one of these days, I can invite she home to meet you.' Pierre was getting carried away by his enthusiasm.

'Boy, you crazy,' his mother was stern. 'You can't invite she here in de day, she'll see you face, and people will laugh at you when she don't want to see you no more.'

'All right, I forget meself.' Pierre shrugged his shoulders. 'In the night, then, when I have a night off, I going to invite she here.'

'Me son, I happy for you, but you mustn't expect too much,' said his mother with resignation.

'I don't know about that,' Pierre laughed. 'I have a feeling that she is the kinda person who like people for what they is and not how they look, and maybe she ugly like me.'

'You don't know that for sure, me son.' His mother had a strange look in her eyes.

'Anyway, at least a woman talking to me, even if she don't know how ugly I is.'

The next night, Pierre sat on the bench at the building site, waiting, anxious and excited. The woman appeared quietly and greeted him, 'Good-night, howdy! It's me, don't shine the light!'

'Oh yes, goodnight, Miss,' Pierre said eagerly. 'How you been keeping yourself?'

'Well, boy, I was thinking of you all the time,' answered the woman, coming close to him and the sweet perfume surrounding and intoxicating him.

'Me too, I was thinking about you all the time,' said Pierre, taking a deep breath. 'You does smell so nice and wonderful. And I tell me mother about you too.'

'That's very nice of you. Maybe I'll meet she sometime.'

'Yes, I was thinking . . .' Pierre stopped, put a hand on his head and said, 'I forgetting me man-ners, you want a seat?'

'No, I all right,' the woman said coolly. 'You was saying?'

'I was thinking that maybe you can come and meet me mother soon. And since you don't like light and brightness, maybe you can come to we home in the night.'

'Yes, that'll be fine,' the woman replied gaily. 'I sure you mother is kind and mannerly like you.'

'Yes, she's very understanding,' said Pierre, his heart pounding as though it was about to explode.

'All you have to remember the important thing,

I don't like light. You must remind you mother about it. Bright light does hurt me eyes bad.'

'I tell she that already, she say it's all right, she not fussy.'

'All right, then, just tell me when you want me to come.'

'The reason I don't want you to come in the day,' said Pierre, bowing his head, 'is the people around here like too much gossip; I don't want them to know me business, they too inquisitive.'

The woman wanted Pierre to trust her completely. 'It's all right, I don't mind coming in the night at all,' she said cheerfully. 'But how is you going to work that out, I mean, you work in the night?'

'That'll be all right. I have a friend who can take over here for me on the night I'll invite you to me home.'

'All right, then, that's settled.' The woman was satisfied. She was carefully laying a trap to catch Pierre.

On the night Pierre invited the woman to his home, his mother had to go to see an ailing friend. Pierre did not plan for this to happen, but it was the only night his friend could cover as watchman for him. Secretly Pierre led the woman to his house, opened the door quietly and showed her in.

'I like you place,' the woman whispered with a sly look on her face.

'Thank you, let me find you a seat.' And Pierre groped around in the darkness until he stumbled into a chair. 'Here, I find one, make youself comfortable.'

'Thank you,' said the woman who did not have any difficulty finding her way in the dark. 'Thank you, I is all right.' And she sat down.

'You want something to drink?' Pierre asked nervously.

'No liquor, though,' the woman answered, relaxing on the chair; 'a little cocoa or ovaltine will be just fine.'

'All right, I going make you some cocoa,' and Pierre groped his way into the kitchen.

The woman began to hum and shake her head from side to side. Pierre fumbled his way out of the kitchen, came back to her and said, 'The water boiling, it going to be ready in a few minutes.'

'You mother does keep this place clean and tidy,' the woman flattered Pierre.

'Yes, me mother does try she best,' Pierre said modestly. 'And, I say again, she was really sorry she couldn't be here to meet you.'

'I tell you already, it's all right. I'll meet she some other time,' the woman said reassuring him.

'Yes, well, let me go and make the cocoa,' Pierre said and groped his way into the kitchen.

Suddenly the front door opened and Pierre's mother came in: her ailing friend had died and in her grief over her friend's death had completely forgotten about her son's guest. Her hand came upon Pierre's torch on a table and she switched it on and the light fell on the woman.

Pierre dropped the cup in the kitchen and looked around wildly.

'Oh God! I forget . . . but who . . . boy, oh God! . . . the woman have cloven hoof! She's La Diablesse! . . . Oh Jesus Christ . . . !' Ma Gautier was screaming.

The woman disappeared. Pierre rushed out to his mother who was hysterical, and looked around for the woman; they then heard a woman's laugh outside and an angry voice shouting: 'If you didn't

put on the light I woulda kill the two of you with kick!'

Pierre was trembling. His mother became calm and slowly said, 'Pierre, boy, I come in, and when I turn on the light me see she sitting there with she legs crossed and I see one of she foot is a cloven foot.'

'That is why she don't like light, she's La Diablesse.' Pierre broke down, cupping his face in his hands. 'Oh God, look what I get meself into, she woulda kill me.'

'Yes, all this time, she planning to kill the two of us,' his mother caught her breath. 'Thank God, I shine the light, thank God.'

Pierre wept bitterly as his mother lit the kerosene-lamp.

SOME CREATIONS

(from Surinam)

PETRONELLA BREINBURG

IN THE beginning, there was only one great God.
This great God was almighty. This great God
created everything except a wife for himself, except assistants. This great God felt at first that he
could cope with all that he created. He could cope
with his sky and sea, the birds and people – with
everything. However, God's creations began to
give him trouble. God soon saw that things would
be easier for him if he had some help. God waved
his arm about and created help. His helpers were
called demi-Gods.

God called his helpers together and gave each
one certain duties. To the first one he said: 'You
over there, you be the ruler of the water. You shall
control everything in water.'

'Thank you, my creator.' The helper bowed and
went away.

'You over there,' God called again, pointing to
another helper, 'you be the ruler of my sky.'

'Thank you, my creator, but to rule a sky as big
as yours I will need helpers,' he replied.

'Are you trying to say you cannot do the work?'
God asked patiently.

'I cannot do it all, my creator, for I am not as

powerful as you are,' said the second assistant who
had long since noticed that God did not give his
helpers as much power as he had himself.

'So you want my power?' said God who was
getting angry.

'No, my creator. I am only asking for help so
that I may carry out my duties to the utmost
perfection,' said the helper.

God did not argue. He knew all. He knew that
the helper was lying. He was not satisfied to be
just an assistant and would very soon want to
overthrow him. There came a long pause because
God never did things hurriedly. Then God waved
his arm about and destroyed that helper at once.

The demi-Gods were stronger than everything;
stronger than man and beast, flower and sea, birds
and fishes, but never as strong as God.

Each demi-God took up his post. The demi-God
of Rain went to control the rain. The demi-God of
Thunder went to control the thunder. The demi-
God of Lightning went to control the lightning,
and so on. All the demi-Gods were happy and often
worked together. There was, however, one helper,
the demi-God of Lightning, who always fretted.

'I want a wife,' he would cry, as he sent his first
light ray flashing through the sky.

'Shut up, idiot!' the demi-God of Thunder would
shout at him.

The people on earth could see the lightning
flashing. The people on earth could hear the
thunderous noise and the people knew that the
demi-God of Thunder and the demi-God of Lightning were rowing again. Sometimes this rowing
would go on and on.

'I want a wife.' The demi-God would flash a light
each time stronger than the last. He would flash

his ray so strongly that the whole world would shudder, man and beast would all run and hide in whatever hiding place they could find.

'Shut up!' the demi-God of Thunder would shout. He was the only demi-God not afraid of the demi-God of Lightning's 'Flash'; he would roar, more loudly each time, and in a language which ordinary humans could not understand.

For a long while the flashing and roaring would carry on until the demi-God of Rain could not bear it any longer. Now, the demi-God of Rain was no weakling though he did not like to fight. Slowly the demi-God of Rain would plead with the demi-God of Thunder and the demi-God of Lightning to stop bickering like ordinary man and beast, like flowers and bees. Only when the two did not stop their arguments would the demi-God of Rain lose his temper and fight. He would often hold the two and push them from each other. He would push and fill their mouths with water, eventually shutting them up, even if it was just for a while.

A long time would pass but sooner or later the demi-God of Lightning would start the quarrel all over again. Each time, the demi-God of Rain would intervene and stop the argument.

One day the demi-God of Lightning had an idea: 'Ah, I will go down to earth and find me a wife.'

He dashed to earth but his ray was so strong that it set most of the earth afire. It had most of the earth's creatures screaming and running with fear. Trees were set alight and the grass caught fire too.

The demi-God of Lightning's disappearance to earth's soil did not go unnoticed by the demi-God of Thunder, who followed at once. His roar, however, and his heavy breathing were too strong for the earth's creatures. So strong were they that

some creatures were deafened. Trees were slashed
in half, flowers were blown into the sky. So strong
was the power of the demi-God of Thunder that
the whole earth would have been destroyed if the
demi-God of Rain had not intervened.

The demi-God of Rain poured water down.
There were floods everywhere. But the fires went
out and the row between the demi-God of Thunder
and the demi-God of Lightning stopped for a
while.

A long time passed. Many moons and suns
came and went. Then the demi-God of Lightning
started his lightning again. This time it was
the earth's creatures who decided to reason with
him.

'Don't destroy us, oh demi-God, helper of the
Almighty. Don't destroy us. We'll give you our
best maidens, best food, our best drink. We'll make
you a great feast and you can dance as much as
you want, but do not destroy us so.'

The demi-God of Lightning liked what he was
hearing. He had always wanted to enjoy that feasting of earth's creatures which so far he had only
seen from a distance. 'Very well,' he said, grinned,
and thought how weak and whimpering earth's
creatures were. His immediate thought was to
make them his slaves. 'Very well,' he replied, 'but
get going at once.' He bullied them, flashing lights
into their eyes and making them run faster than
the wind.

Earth's creatures wanted to make the demi-God
of Lightning happy. The creatures went into the
forest and chopped down a young but very strong
tree. The creatures took the best part of the tree
trunk and made it hollow. They then killed a
young but strong deer, took the hide, washed and

cleaned it, and strapped it over the hollow tree trunk. This was the earth's very first *Apinti drum*.*

When the earth's creatures beat the Apinti drum, they thought it did not sound nice enough, so they went back into the forest. Again they chopped down a young but strong tree. Again they took the best part of the trunk and made it hollow. Again they killed a young but strong deer, and cleaned and washed the hide, then strapped it over the hollow trunk. That was the earth's second Apinti drum. When the earth's creatures beat the two Apinti drums, they found that they sounded better together but still not very nice.

So once more the earth's creatures went straight to the forest, chopped a young but strong tree, took the best part of the trunk and made it hollow, killed a young but strong deer, cleaned and washed the hide, then strapped it over the hollow tree. When the earth's creatures beat the first and the second and the third Apinti drums together, they found that they sounded beautiful indeed. The creatures got food, drink and dancing maidens ready.

Among the maidens of the village was Eliza. No one invited her because they did not think that she was beautiful, but Eliza had to help look after the other maidens and stand them in a row to be chosen from by the elders.

The maiden chosen was the most beautiful on earth. To prepare her for the big occasion, she was washed in beautiful scented flower water. She was wrapped from the waist down with the most beautiful loin cloth. Her hair was combed and her

---

* *Apinti drum*: an African drum, used in religious ceremonies

young breasts were painted until she looked fit to be the wife of the demi-God of Lightning.

On the night of the feast, the maiden was placed on an intricately carved rosewood stool. Her brothers beat out beautiful rhythms from the three Apinti drums. Her sisters sang haunting songs. So the drums beat and the voices sang until the demi-God of Lightning, who had by now been named Sofia-abada by the earth's creatures, dashed down to earth.

Sofia-abada was disappointed, for as soon as the maiden saw the flash of lightning coming towards her, she became so frightened that she fell down and all her life went from her. Sofia-abada was sad indeed, and felt guilty about causing the maiden to lose her life. Because Sofia-abada felt guilty, he became very angry. He roared and shouted and stamped about until all the earth's creatures ran and hid.

Because the earth's creatures were afraid that Sofia-abada would destroy them, they very soon prepared another feast. This time they had three maidens all fit to be Sofia-abada's wife. Now Sofia-abada did not frighten his brides, he just watched them dance for him. First he danced with one maiden. He did not want to take her life, so when she became tired, he let her sit and rest. Sofia-abada then danced with the second maiden. When he had danced until he felt that the maiden needed rest, he left her. Sofia-abada then went to dance with the third maiden. He had had plenty to eat, plenty to drink and had danced with three maidens, yet he was not tired. 'Where are the other maidens?' he bellowed angrily.

Now Sofia-abada wanted to see all the maidens in the village. The earth's creatures became really frightened and ran around chanting Sofia-abada's name because they could not find any more beautiful maidens. The chant would start with one voice calling the name once, then a chorus chanting the name three times, one time for each maiden. The chant would start very loudly and end very softly with a note of pleading in it. It went something like this:

> *One voice:*
> 'Sofia-abada, ho jah jah hej.'
>
> *Chorus:*
> 'Sofia-abada ho jah jah hej,
> Sofia-abada ho jah jah hej,
> Sofia-abada ho jah jah hej.'

While the earth's creatures chanted in loud voices, the drummers beat the Apinti drums until the earth began to crack under the sound, and all the creatures began to dance as if in a trance. Finally, at midnight, Sofia-abada came back. This time he did not dance, he spoke to the earth's creatures. He said: 'You have not brought out all your maidens, you have hidden one. For the last time, I want to see all the maidens or I'll destroy everything.'

The earth's creatures begged and begged. They said that they did not really have any other maidens and begged not to be destroyed. It was then that Eliza came forward and spoke. Eliza was dirty and wet from fetching water from the creek. But she spoke. She spoke before any of the earth's creatures could stop her. She said that there were no other young maidens left. She was the only young female but she was not for a great demi-God like Sofia-abada. She could not be his wife but she

would like to go away and live in the sky. She
would work hard and do anything. If Sofia-abada
promised to leave the earth's creatures alone, she
would go away and clean the sky and work very
hard.

The earth's creatures were shocked. No one had
ever dared to speak to the demi-God of Lightning
in that manner. No one had dared to confront the
demi-God before.

The earth's creatures were ready to apologize
for Eliza, but for the first time the demi-God of
Lightning showed kindness and seemed pleased.
He told Eliza that she did not have to go away into
the sky. She could stay where she was and he
promised not to destroy the earth, not even when
he was very angry and rowed with the demi-God
of Thunder. He would never set the earth alight.

He then made his way back to where he came
from. The earth's creatures were pleased. They
sang happy songs and danced. They beat the Apinti
drums and danced to them. Someone said that
Eliza should be made a princess and later, when
she grew up, even a queen of the earth. But Eliza
refused. She went as usual to fetch water from the
nearby creek. She sang happily as she went. She
knew that Sofia-abada would not destroy the earth
no matter how much lightning and thunder there
was.

TOEWI AND KROEMOE

(from Curaçao)

PETRONELLA BREINBURG

M ANY YEARS ago, long before the Europeans invaded the islands and other parts around the Caribbean Sea, there lived a very beautiful girl. Some said that she was of the Arawak tribe while others said she was of the Caiquetio tribe which was very different. One thing everyone was sure about was that the girl, named Toewi, was very beautiful. She was the most beautiful creature in the whole area. Her skin was golden brown as if gold dust had been rubbed on it. Her hair was black and long and she always plaited it in such a way that it looked as if she had two long black snakes hanging down her back or dangling from side to side when she ran.

Toewi was very happy but she was not allowed to play too far away from the place where she lived. She was not allowed to let any stranger talk to her either.

One of Toewi's favourite games was pretending. She often pretended that she had travelled far, far away across the wide sea where the grown men went to fish. She would pretend that she met the rain-god and talked to him. She would ask him nicely not to let it rain. She always pretended that the rain-god listened to her and did as she asked.

Toewi always pretended when her parents went out and left her alone. Her mother often went out to gather roots with the other women and her father went fishing with other men.

On one occasion, Toewi's parents had again gone away for the day. She was left at home to weave cloth or just to play after she had finished her chores and had eaten. Toewi sang softly while weaving the cloth. She was again pretending that she was somewhere else. She was pretending that she was flying high above the blue sea, again to the home of the rain-god.

So busy was Toewi with weaving, humming and pretending, that it was a long time before she noticed that a young man had come to stand by the doorway.

'Oh, eh, my parents are away and you can't come in, eh.' The young man just smiled. Toewi thought that he was handsome. He was dressed in all the fineries of a young warrior. And if he was a young warrior, then he could not be a rain-god because the rain-god did not fight and the rain-god was old, very old with a very long beard. Toewi spoke again and repeated what she had said before.

'My people are away, you must come back when they return.' The young warrior spoke, 'Don't be afraid, I've come to take you away.' Toewi stared. For a while she could not speak. The young warrior may well be a chief's son, judging from his head-dress, but she could not go with him. She should not even be talking to him. She must not talk to strangers. But she did talk. 'You must leave now. Come back when my father is at home,'

she said. The young man did not speak again;
instead, he disappeared just as suddenly as he
had come.

Toewi thought she had pretended that all this
had happened and she smiled, thinking it had been
a good 'pretend' game. Since Toewi never told
anyone about her pretend games, she did not talk
about the handsome young man, not at first,
anyway.

On the next day, Toewi had to fetch water from
the river. She loved to fetch water from the river.
She enjoyed sitting down for a while and singing.
She would sing softly and beautifully as she played
with the water. Toewi was singing again that day,
when suddenly, the same young warrior appeared
in front of her. Again, the handsome young man
did not speak at first. He just stood there and
smiled.

Toewi spoke first. She had completely forgotten
that she was not to talk to strangers. She said, 'I
am not seeing you. Eh, eh, you're in my pretend
game. You don't really exist, that's it, you're in
my pretending game.'

The young man did not reply. He simply stepped
forward and helped Toewi put the earthen jug on
her head. Toewi remembered then that she was
not allowed to talk to strangers. But she also remembered that this young warrior was only a
person in her pretend game. The handsome young
man followed Toewi. Then he spoke. 'Do you still
believe that I am not real?'

'Eh, eh,' Toewi tried but failed to find something
to say. The handsome young man disappeared once
again.

The next day, Toewi again went to fetch water
from the river. This time she waited to see if the

young warrior would appear again. It was a long time before he finally appeared. This time the handsome young man sat by the river and talked to Toewi. After that day, Toewi eagerly went to the river to fetch water. Every day the handsome young man appeared. Every day the handsome young man and Toewi talked. Every day Toewi reminded herself that he was only a person in her pretend game, so she could talk to him.

One day Toewi and Kroemoe, the handsome young warrior, were talking. Suddenly a flock of crows flew over their heads. The flock of crows made a terrible noise. Toewi picked up a stone and angrily threw it at the flock. 'Stupid crows,' she muttered. 'Don't do that,' said the young warrior, angrily. 'They're only crows,' explained Toewi, sad because she had angered him. 'Never throw stones at crows,' said Kroemoe, angrily, and at once disappeared. Toewi pleaded, 'Come back, Kroemoe. Please, please come back, you're my friend . . . please come back!' But Kroemoe did not come back. So, sadly, Toewi went home. When Toewi got home, she cried. She did not have many friends and even if the young warrior was only in her pretend game, he was friendly. He was handsome and he was a warrior, and maybe even a chief's son.

The next day Toewi went again to fetch water. Toewi sang sadly on her way to the river. She sat down by the river and sang sadly to the river. What if the young man was a river spirit? No, he couldn't be. He could be a sky spirit, she thought, and waited for a long time. But the handsome young man never appeared that day. Nor the next day, nor the next. Each day Toewi went to the river to fetch water. Each day Toewi sang by the river and waited. 'Oh, why did I throw stones at the crows? Maybe he likes crows. I'll never throw stones at crows again, please come back.' The handsome young man did not appear.

After many days and weeks, a very unhappy Toewi got ill. The medicine man was called in. He tried his best but Toewi remained ill and unhappy and refused to eat. Three more medicine men were called. They all tried. They made a feast for Toewi. They danced, sang and prayed. But none of the medicine men made Toewi better. Toewi's mother and father got ill too, because they were worried about Toewi, their only child. All the people in the village came to Toewi's house. All the people sang and danced because Toewi was the prettiest creature around. They all danced and prayed. Yet Toewi stayed ill. The people sang to all the gods. And still Toewi stayed ill. The people danced for all the gods. But none of it helped. Instead, Toewi was dying.

The villagers were upset. 'She's dying, she's dying,' they all moaned and cried, 'our Toewi is dying.' The villagers did not want Toewi to die. 'Get her on her feet,' said the women and helped Toewi to stand up. 'Get her to sing.' The women sang and tried to make Toewi join in. Toewi was trying to sing for the last time. She made a last effort. Toewi tried really hard. She sang beautifully. She sang about her pretend games and the rain-god. She sang about the handsome warrior of her game. Suddenly Kroemoe appeared in the doorway. Kroemoe was wearing all the fineries of a chief, a young chief. 'There, there,' Toewi whispered. 'He's there!' But Kroemoe disappeared just as suddenly. 'He came back,' said Toewi. 'Who came?' asked the women in turn. They had not seen the young warrior.

Toewi began to get better. She began to be happy again. She began to sing again. Soon Toewi was well enough to be left alone. Soon she was well enough to do chores, such as fetching water. Toewi went to the river every day to fetch water. She sang every day. Every day Kroemoe appeared. Every day Kroemoe and Toewi talked. He told her that his name was Kroemoe and that he came from a place far away.

Kroemoe and Toewi were talking by the river one day when a flock of crows came flying past. Toewi began to speak, 'I won't Kroe —' She had wanted to say that she wouldn't throw stones at them. Kroemoe put his hand over Toewi's mouth, very quickly. Kroemoe seemed frightened. He said, 'Never, never call out my name when there are crows,' his voice trembling. Kroemoe was very frightened.

Many weeks passed. Every day Toewi and Kroemoe talked by the river. Every day a flock of crows would fly past. Sometimes one or two of the flock of crows would sit on the trees by the river. Often Toewi thought that these crows were strange. They were black like other crows, but there was something strange about their beaks. They seemed to have yellow beaks. And their eyes were almost human. Sometimes they frightened her just a little.

One day, Toewi and Kroemoe were talking by the river, when again a flock of crows flew past. She counted them. There were exactly four. Two had red beaks and two had yellow beaks. One very big crow flew very low and came very close to Toewi. Its eyes peered into Toewi's. Toewi stared

because she was afraid of that big crow. 'Kroemoe!' screamed a frightened Toewi, 'Kroemoe!' She dashed towards Kroemoe. Then suddenly it happened. Toewi stared. Kroemoe was turned into a big black crow right before her eyes. 'Kroemoe, Kroemoe, Kroemoe,' Toewi screamed again and again. Suddenly the big black crow grabbed Toewi with its yellow beak. 'No! no!' Toewi cried, but the crow flew away with her. The big black crow had Toewi with him in the tree. Toewi was screaming louder and louder as she was being carried away. All the people of the village heard Toewi's screaming.

The people ran to the river where Toewi went to fetch water. People shouted and screamed and shot arrows into the tree. 'Don't kill it!' shouted Toewi, 'it's Kroemoe, it's really a warrior!' The big black crow did not let go of Toewi. He hugged Toewi gently but lightly as he flew away with her. Toewi was never seen again.

No one is very sure, but people believe that Kroemoe was a crow who took human shape. Or did the crows turn a human into a crow? Was Kroemoe a crow and was it his tribe who wanted him to stop taking human shape? Or could Kroemoe not stop because he loved Toewi?

Some people believe that Kroemoe and Toewi sometimes appear as two big stars in the sky. People also say that Toewi and Kroemoe sometimes, maybe once a year or so, appear as two strange-looking crows with a flock of black crows. No one is sure what really happened, but children love the tale of Toewi and Kroemoe. Some village children even say that when they have gone to fetch water by the black water river they have

seen two strange black crows, one with a
red beak and one with a yellow beak, sitting
nearby and watching with strange, almost human
eyes.

HOW GREASYMAN SPOIL OLD YEAR'S NIGHT

(from Aruba)

SHIRLEY INNIS

GREASYMAN is a ghost-like figure with three forms; one is human, another is what appears to be a huge, shiny ball which engulfs its victims, and the third is not seen but one can hear it by the loud noise it makes when passing. Greasyman comes out at nights to scare people and catch children to give to the Devil.

In the Caribbean, there is a little country called Aruba. In Aruba, there are several kinds of celebrations – Christmas, Carnival, Easter, *Watapana*,* but the most enjoyable of all is 'Old Year's Night'.

A long time ago, there were two little girls who lived in Aruba with their parents and sister Bag-a-Bones and brother Egg-Head-Fred. These two little girls were very naughty and became known to all as Redhead Annie and Purple Judas.

Purple Judas loved to visit her friends, and had no time to do her homework or the daily chores which her parents had given her. At school she always got into trouble with the teachers and

---

* *Watapana*: an annual fund-raising festival

children, because she loved to fight. Greasyman knew all about her.

Redhead Annie did whatever Purple Judas told her. She did not fight because she was too afraid of being beaten up. Therefore, she would always report to Purple Judas when anyone tried to start any trouble with her. Both girls usually planned ahead for the next mischief.

On Old Year's Night, every house would be cleaned, plenty of food would be bought, and everyone was expected to have some money in their hands for good luck. At twelve midnight, the horn from the Oil Refinery would blow for about half an hour; the Chinese did a fireworks display which lasted for an hour, and there were steelbands playing through the streets.

One year, the two girls' parents told them that they were not to go out when the steelbands came. They were warned that if they went they would be left outside for the Greasyman. This made them very unhappy, so they decided to go to bed.

The next day they decided that they could not survive without any mischief, and therefore set about planning how to get out of their home on Old Year's Night without being noticed. But their parents suspected that they would not be able to resist this major celebration and asked Bag-a-Bones and Egg-Head-Fred to follow Redhead Annie and Purple Judas around.

Soon Old Year's Day arrived. The two naughty girls grew more and more restless. By seven o'clock in the evening, every time Redhead Annie got up, Bag-a-Bones would follow her. Every time Purple Judas got up, Egg-Head-Fred would follow her. Soon the two followers became bored with their

role and refused to carry on with it. This was, of
course, ideal for the two naughty little girls.

Greasyman in the form of a shining ball knew
what the girls were thinking and set a trap for
them. At five to twelve midnight, Redhead Annie
and Purple Judas went and sat outside on the porch
as they knew that the Fiesta was about to start.
They played happily together to give their parents
the idea that they were just playing on the porch.

Eventually, neighbours were dashing out of their
houses, the horn was blowing, bells were ringing,
the fireworks started, and steelbands were playing.
The two little girls forgot all about the Greasyman
and rushed out on to the street in search of the
steelband. When they found it, they danced in the
midst of all the crowd until the music stopped an
hour later. They were so very happy that they sang
and danced their way home without even sparing
a thought for the Greasyman.

Suddenly, they heard footsteps behind. They
looked around and saw something shining – it
was Greasyman; he grabbed them both, but they
managed to slip away from him. He continued to
chase them and soon Redhead Annie was caught.
Purple Judas did not look back to see where Redhead Annie was or why she was crying. Greasyman
was on the way to take Redhead Annie to the
Devil. Purple Judas arrived home screaming, 'Let
me in! Let me in!' but her parents wouldn't.
'Please, mother, Greasyman has taken Redhead
Annie!' Her parents jumped up, opened the door
and called the neighbours out. 'Please, Greasyman
has taken Redhead Annie! Help!' they cried.

The neighbours came rushing out to help. They
looked and looked. Meanwhile, Greasyman had
been singing and dancing, and saying, 'I've got

Redhead Annie, I've got Redhead Annie! She won't be seeing her parents again!' Eventually, he stopped, hid Redhead Annie and told her, 'I'm going to get the Devil and he's going to eat you up.' Redhead Annie cried and hid her face in her hands.

After searching for a long while, some neighbours heard someone crying in an alley-way. When they got closer to the crying, they could see the figure of a little girl curled up. It was Redhead Annie. They tried touching her and she screamed, 'Go away! Grea . . . Grea . . . Greasyman! I want to go home!' They took her up and told her that they were taking her home. She was so frightened that she was speechless and rigid with fear. The whole neighbourhood went to Redhead Annie's house telling her parents how everybody's Old Year's Night was spoilt.

From then on the girls never joined in the celebrations again.

EXPLANATORY NOTES

Me Camoudi by Grace Nichols (p.34)
This tale has its roots in the trickster
mythology like that of Anancy the cunning
spider-man. The Camoudi is a type of
boa-constrictor who ambushes its prey. It is
so cunning that many people believe it
possesses human guile.

The Gaulin Wife by Patricia Glinton (p.48)
In Bahamian folklore, the *Gaulin* or
Gaulding changes into human form to
seduce and kill the opposite sex.

The Ibelles and the Lost Paths by Pedro
Pérez Sarduy (p.75)
Of all the African peoples, the Yoruba tribe
of Nigeria made the greatest literary impact
on Cuba. The tale of the *ibeyi* or *ibelles*
(twins) is told in various ways and is similar
in aim to Yoruba mythology in that its
protagonists are human beings, and there is
always a moral to the story.

The Coquí and Gabriel by Alfredo Arango
Franco (p.85)
This tale is based on myths about the coquí,
which is a little frog that only lives in Puerto
Rico, and dies if it leaves Puerto Rico. The
coquí is one of the most representative
symbols of Puerto Rico. It has been

traditionally associated with Puerto Rican national identity. The tale is also related to slavery and black consciousness in the island.

Maichack by Soraya Bermejo   (p.96)
Based on a legend told by the Camaracoto Indians of Venezuela

The Elf-Stone by Jean Popeau   (p.106)
In the Dominican Republic and Haiti, people believe there is an elf-stone which can be obtained from wells deep in the forest where elves live. The elf-stone is formed in the shape of a man or a woman or an animal, by the effect of many years of rain wearing it away. In order to obtain the stone you must walk deep into the forest. It is believed that you can 'call the man you love' or perform other magic actions with the elf-stone. It is guarded by the elves. You must not upset them; if they ask you a question you must give the right answer, otherwise they might throw stones at you.

The Little Girl Saved by her Father by Alex-Louise Tessonneau   (p.117)
A *Galipot* is an evil blood-sucking invisible spirit that haunts the midnight hour. A bush-bath may protect children from its invisible fangs. They are a threat to new-born babies, so that midwives give babies a bush-bath, or put a bundled-up bottle near the baby to trick the evil spirit.

The Devil's Agent by Jean Popeau   (p.128)

Maskalili is a servant of the devil: his job is
to make sure that humans keep promises
made to the chief devil. They make their
bargains with the chief through him. He is
the height of a four-year-old child, with feet
turned over so that the toes point backwards,
and the heels forwards in order to confuse
hunters who may be chasing him.

The Woman in Black by Jean Popeau
(p.138)
Certain sorcerers, like the bocor, have the
power to cause sudden death, and then
bring the dead back to life again, even after
burial. These half-conscious beings are
zombies, and are under the command of the
bocor. Zombies are made to work like slaves,
and are fed food which contains no salt.
Families who are suspicious of the sudden
death of a relative put a knife in the heart
of the dead person, or cut off some vital part.
This prevents the dead from becoming a
zombie.

Pierre and the La Diablesse by Faustin
Charles   (p.148)
The myth of the La Diablesse or
devil-woman is popular in the
French-speaking Caribbean, and some
English-speaking territories as well. La
Diablesse is a beautiful woman who lures
men to their death. She has a human foot and
a cloven hoof which is hidden because she
always wears long dresses. She is afraid of
bright lights and only appears at night.

Some Creations by Petronella Breinburg
(p.159)
This is a tale told to children in villages in
Surinam to assure them that lightning and
thunder cannot hurt them. It is a Creole
tale, which would normally be told in
deep-Sranan, the local dialect.